Pirates of
Quentaris

THE QUENTARIS CHRONICLES

Pirates of Quentaris

Sherryl Clark

Series editors: Michael Pryor and Paul Collins

Lothian
BOOKS

To Brian, bush pirate.

Lothian Books
An imprint of Time Warner Book Group Australia
132 Albert Road, South Melbourne, Victoria 3205
www.lothian.com.au

First published 2006

National Library of Australia
Cataloguing-in-Publication data:

Clark, Sherryl.
Pirates of Quentaris

For children.
ISBN 0 7344 0883 8.

1. Pirates — Juvenile fiction. I. Title. (Series: Quentaris chronicles).

A823.3

Cover artwork by Jeremy Reston
Map by Jeremy Maitland-Smith
Original map by Marc McBride
Cover and text design by John van Loon
Printed in Australia by Griffin Press

Contents

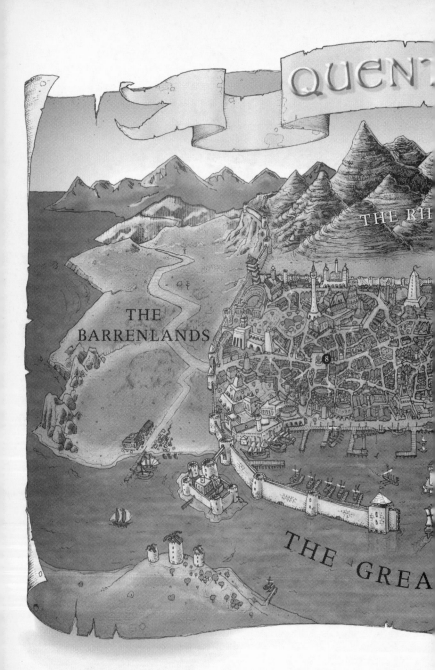

QUENT

THE RII

THE
BARRENLANDS

8

THE GREA

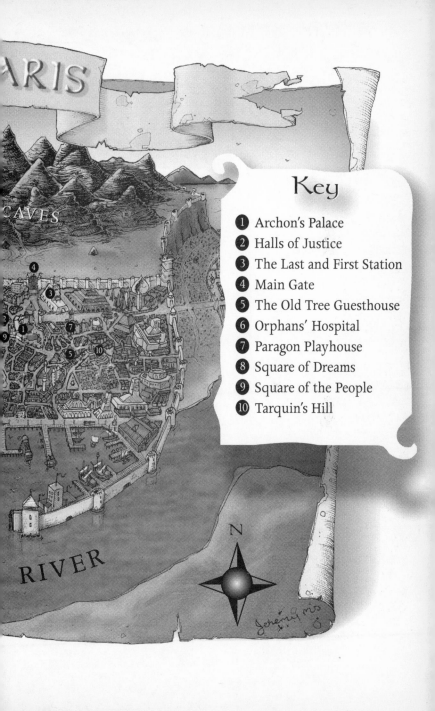

ARIS

CAVES

RIVER

Key

1 Archon's Palace
2 Halls of Justice
3 The Last and First Station
4 Main Gate
5 The Old Tree Guesthouse
6 Orphans' Hospital
7 Paragon Playhouse
8 Square of Dreams
9 Square of the People
10 Tarquin's Hill

1
Dawn
Raid

KIALL GROANED IN HIS sleep and flung one
arm above his head. The nightmare held
him in its grip — he was trapped in a
dark hole with chains around his wrists and ankles,
then somewhere a door banged and a hand grabbed
his arm.

'Kiall! Wake up!' The hand shook him hard and
slowly the chains dissolved. He opened his eyes and,
seeing only a dim shape, panicked for a moment.

'Kiall!' It was his twin sister, Maya, proving he was no longer in the hole.

'What? Whatsa matter?' Kiall struggled to sit up, and heard shouting and banging coming from below.

'It's Papa. The City Watch is arresting him. You must come.' Maya didn't move back fast enough and Kiall stood on her foot as he leapt out of bed. She only grunted and pushed him ahead of her as she raced back downstairs.

In the hallway, two guards held Kiall's father tightly while their sergeant fastened metal bands around his wrists. Paolo had not gone easily — a vase lay in shards on the tiled floor and a painting hung askew. Kiall's mother, Ysabel, stood in her nightgown, holding a candle that guttered in the draught from the open front door. 'Why are you arresting him?' she cried. 'He's not a criminal.'

'Shouldn't have put up a fight then, should he?' the sergeant snapped.

'What do you expect?' Paolo said, wincing at the tight bands. 'Barging into our house before dawn. I thought you were robbers.'

The sergeant snorted and pushed Paolo towards the door.

'Stop!' Kiall leapt down the last three stairs and grabbed his father, trying to pull him away from the guards. 'You're not taking him anywhere.'

The sergeant shoved Kiall back and half-drew his sword. 'Stay out of this, boy, or you'll be going with him.'

'Don't you threaten —' Kiall's fist rose up, and Maya screamed, 'No!' Ysabel quickly grabbed his arm.

'Quiet, Kiall, you'll only make it worse,' she said. 'We'll follow them to the Halls of Justice and sort this out. These guards are just doing their job.'

The sergeant glared at Kiall before signalling the others to haul Paolo out through the front door and down the street.

Kiall turned to his mother. 'Why have they arrested him?' he demanded. 'He's done nothing.' Of course Papa was innocent. But why did his mother suddenly look so old and worn?

'It's the business,' she said slowly, sagging into the gold-embossed chair behind her. 'There have been so many things go wrong. The ships sinking, the fire ...'

'Papa said it would be all right,' Kiall said. 'He said he'd arranged a loan.'

Ysabel grimaced. 'It would have been his fourth, and the lender refused. Said he'd heard Paolo's ships had been sabotaged. Bad luck is one thing, but being deliberately put out of business made him too much of a risk.'

Maya sat on the bottom step, her long black hair falling across her face as she stared at the floor. 'Do you mean the fire was deliberate too?'

'I don't know,' Ysabel said. 'Maybe.'

'Then we have to find out who's doing it,' Kiall said. 'And demand compensation.'

Ysabel rubbed her face. 'If it were that easy, your father would have already done so.'

'We can't just sit here and do nothing,' Kiall said.

Ysabel got up and shut the front door. 'Of course not. We will go to the Halls of Justice and see what is going on.'

'We'll go and bring him home, that's what we'll do!' Kiall said hotly.

'Don't be silly,' Ysabel said. 'We won't be helping him if we cause a fuss. These things must be done the correct way.'

Correct way! Kiall wanted to race to the Halls of Justice and demand they let his father go. Didn't they know who he was? He was the famous Paolo

Tigran, the rift adventurer who'd made his fortune by finding a sapphire mine and bringing back the finest gems that Quentaris had ever seen. And now he was one of the most astute merchants in the city, with a fleet of his own ships. Or he had been, until a series of misfortunes had decimated the fleet.

This arrest was a mistake — it had to be. They would sort it out and Paolo would be home by midday, at the latest.

Kiall stomped upstairs to get dressed, then refused breakfast, pacing the hallway until Ysabel and Maya were ready. They set off to the Halls of Justice as the pink dawn-light cast grey shadows under the walls. Paolo would be in the dungeons beneath the Halls of Justice, waiting for the first morning session of the courts. Surely, Kiall thought, the case would be immediately dismissed.

They were not allowed down to the dungeons to talk to Paolo so Ysabel was forced to give the bundle of clean clothes and breakfast food to one of the guards, hoping he would be honest enough to put it into Paolo's hands. She would have bribed him with a few copper rounds, but she had none to spare. Before leaving, they'd scoured the house for money and only found two silver moons. It was barely enough to feed them for a week; they couldn't afford to give away even a few rounds right now.

They sat in the designated court and waited for Paolo's case to be called. It took over an hour — first they watched a series of petty thieves, drunks and brawlers whisked in and out, each receiving a standard fine and sent on his or her way. Kiall sat in his seat, simmering with rage, barely able to contain himself. At last the case was announced in a booming voice by the clerk.

'The Eminent Tash Morley versus Paolo Tigran. The charge is criminal bankruptcy.'

'What's going on?' Ysabel muttered. 'Why are the bank or the merchants not mentioned? What is this charge?'

Kiall paled as his father was brought in. Even from where they sat, he could see the large bruise on Paolo's face and the way he limped.

'What is criminal bankruptcy?' Maya whispered.

'I have never heard of it,' Ysabel said. 'Ssh now.'

The judge peered at the papers in front of him, then down at Paolo who stood as straight as he could, his head held high. At least he had received the clean clothes. To stand in the court in his night-clothes would have looked very bad.

'Criminal bankruptcy is a serious charge,' said the judge. 'The first I have adjudicated over. Is the plaintiff here in court?'

'I am, your honour.'

Kiall jerked around and saw the speaker behind him. Tash Morley wore a dark green satin coat and around his neck hung the thick gold chain and medallion that adorned him as chief of the market. It was rumoured that Morley's gold came principally from bribes rather than the shops and stalls he owned.

'Viper!' Ysabel whispered.

'Do you understand the seriousness of the charge?' asked the judge.

'I do, your honour,' Morley said. 'I represent several of the largest merchants in Quentaris. This man owes not hundreds, but thousands, of royals, and has deliberately swindled us out of our money. Therefore it is more than common bankruptcy.'

'It was not deliberate!' Paolo shouted. 'My ships sank, my warehouses were set on fire. How is that my fault?'

'Quiet!' The judge banged his gavel half a dozen times while Morley smirked.

'Your honour, may I speak?' Ysabel had risen and moved forward.

'Are you this man's lawyer?' the judge asked.

'No, your honour, I am his wife.'

'Then you will have nothing useful to contribute.' The judge glanced at the papers again. 'I find that the evidence provided here is amply sufficient to bind Paolo Tigran over for trial without bail. I suggest, Tigran, that you hire the best lawyer you can afford.'

Kiall jumped up from his seat. 'How are we supposed to do that?' he shouted. 'We have no money.'

'Why don't you use some of the gold your father has hidden?' Morley said.

'Are you crazy?' Kiall spat. 'He hasn't stolen a single round.'

'He's a common thief, not even good enough to be in the Thieves' Guild,' Morley sneered. 'By the looks of you, you should be in the dungeons, too.'

Kiall's rage rose to white heat; he leapt over the wooden rail and ran towards Morley, wanting only to plant his fist in the man's mouth and shut him up.

The judge's gavel crashed down over and over again. 'Guards! Clear the court!'

As two officials hustled Ysabel and Maya back, Kiall was seized and bundled out through the doors, then dumped on the marble steps outside. One of the guards took the opportunity to kick him in the ribs and laughed as he doubled over. Kiall lay on the cold stone, bruised and humiliated, ignoring his mother's shocked cries. Tash Morley had disappeared, no doubt to tell his cronies that Paolo was back in the dungeon.

Maya tried to help Kiall get up but he shrugged her off, sitting up on his own. 'Stop fussing,' he snapped. 'We have to do something — now.'

'Like what?' Maya said. 'Punch Morley? How will that help?'

Ysabel sat on a bench, her head in her hands. 'I keep the accounts. I know Paolo hasn't been swindling them. And I know there is no money left. Not even for a lawyer.'

'Can't we ask Papa's friends?' Kiall said.

She shook her head. 'He has already borrowed from them. Now they have closed their doors to us.'

'What about your jewellery?' Maya asked. Paolo had given Ysabel many fine pieces over the years, beginning with the first sapphire necklace that he had brought back through the rift caves.

'Sold months ago,' Ysabel said bitterly. 'Our so-called business friends in the market offered us a pittance.'

'I don't understand,' Kiall said. 'Papa is not a terrible businessman. How could *all* of his money and merchandise be gone?'

'After seeing Morley in court this morning, I am growing more and more suspicious.' Ysabel stood. 'But I can prove nothing and trying to will only waste time. I need to find money for a lawyer and more money for the extras.'

'Extras?' Maya said.

'Bribes,' Ysabel said flatly. 'Morley has been bribed into this and it is probably the only way out for Paolo.'

'Why can't we just go and threaten Morley?' Kiall said.

Ysabel shook her head. 'No. We will not lower ourselves to their level. Now try putting your brain to useful work and think of someone who will lend us a few royals.'

She stalked off, heading for their house, and Kiall and Maya trailed behind.

'There must be a way to solve this,' Maya said. 'I will try to think of a plan.'

'You and your plans,' Kiall scoffed. 'Action is what we need. I'd like to sneak into Morley's house one night and steal back Papa's gold.'

'We are in enough trouble already.'

'Well, I'm not going to walk around Quentaris, begging for a round here and a round there. I've had a better idea of how to find the money we need.'

'Like what?'

'The rift caves,' Kiall said. 'That's how Papa made his first fortune. Why shouldn't I do the same?'

'You forget — the Archon has banned anyone from going into the caves for three months.' Maya glanced over her shoulder at the ever-present cliffs beyond the city. 'That earthquake made a lot of the caves unstable. No one is allowed in until the guides have verified they are safe again.'

'That's stupid,' Kiall said. 'The caves are never completely safe. That's what the guides are for.'

Maya shrugged. 'There's your other problem, don't you see? If we don't have any money for Papa's lawyer, we certainly have none for a rift guide either. So you might as well do what Mama asked.'

'Don't you ever get sick of being sensible?' Kiall snapped.

Maya grinned and thumped him on the arm. 'You should try it some time. You might find it helpful.'

'Hmph.' He didn't find being sensible to be any use at all. And it tended to make life downright boring. He shoved his clenched hands deep into his pockets and kept walking, head down. He'd keep his ideas to himself from now on, and Maya and Mama would be the last people he'd tell.

2
Unwanted
Advice

BY THE TIME HE reached their home, Kiall's stomach was grumbling so loudly that he had to eat before setting out again. His mother gave him two slices of bread and a piece of cheese. 'Get used to it,' she said. 'We might not be able to afford even cheese soon.'

He ate quickly, barely tasting the food, his mind whirling as he discarded several of his original ideas, finally settling on the one he liked. Yes, he liked it a lot. And he knew just who to ask for help and information. He went to his room, brushed his black hair and tied it back, and put on his best white shirt.

'I'm going to visit someone,' he told his mother and Maya.

'Someone with money?' Ysabel asked.

'Yes, it is,' he said. But that wasn't the reason for the visit. Kiall Tigran begged nobody for money.

After asking directions in the street, he eventually arrived at his destination, a three-storey building near the Old Tree Guesthouse. This building held the office of Quentaris's most famous rift guide — Rad de La'rel — but Kiall knew he couldn't afford Rad's services. These days Rad was so famous that only royalty could pay his rates. No, Kiall wanted information and he was hoping Rad would give it for free if he were buttered up enough.

The large brass doors were open, but a short dark man sat in the entrance cleaning his fingernails with a dagger. He glanced at Kiall. 'State your business.'

Kiall gulped. 'I'm here to see Rad de La'rel.'

'He's not seeing nobody. Caves are closed.'

'This is not about hiring him as a guide.'

The man snorted. 'Yer wouldn't have a hope.'

'I just want to talk to him.' Kiall felt sweat break out on his forehead. How stupid would he look if he couldn't even get up the stairs. No, he had to see the guide. He wouldn't give up. His idea was good, if a little foolhardy. Even he had enough sense to know when a plan was risky.

A young red-haired woman came down the stairs behind the guard and stopped, staring at Kiall. 'Who's this?'

'Just some youngster who wants to meet Rad. Want to be a rift guide when you grow up, do you?'

Kiall's face burned and he stepped forward, grabbing the guard by the front of his shirt. 'What business is it of yours?'

In an instant, the man's dagger was at Kiall's throat and he felt its tip pierce the skin. 'Guarding this door is my business,' the man said. 'Especially from the likes of you.'

'Let him go, Wickle,' the woman said. 'He's just a boy.'

When Wickle released him, Kiall didn't step back. 'I've had fifteen birthdays,' he said. 'I'm not a boy.'

'More like a stubborn calf,' she said, smiling at last. 'What do you want with Rad?'

'I need to ask him about something.'

'What?'

He could see she wasn't going to let him past without an explanation. He sighed. 'Sky pirates.'

'What?' She laughed. 'You're not one of those who dreams of being Quentaris's next *hero*, are you?'

'No, I'm not,' Kiall said stiffly.

'Tulcia! Where's my honey cake?' The voice bellowed down the stairs.

'Oh, for —' Tulcia threw up her hands. 'Why don't you go out and find yourself a job sweeping dung?' she bellowed back. 'It's all you're good for.'

She scowled at Wickle and Kiall. 'One of these days I'll quit,' she said. 'Then he'll be sorry.' She grabbed Kiall by the arm and pushed him up the stairs. 'Go up there and ask him your silly questions. His problem is that he's been bored to death since the caves were closed. You might entertain him for an hour or two. Go on.' She gave him another push and then walked off.

Kiall looked at Wickle, who said, 'You heard her. Up you go.'

A few minutes later, Kiall was in Rad's office, wishing he'd thought more clearly about what questions he wanted to ask.

Rad stood by the window, watching the street below and tapping his fingers on the sill. He turned and frowned when he saw Kiall. 'No, I don't take on apprentices, so you're wasting your time.'

'I don't want to be an apprentice,' Kiall said. 'I just wanted to ask you …'

'For what? Money? A donation for something? Pah!' Rad turned back to the window, but this time his eyes focused on the rift caves in the distance. 'Go away.'

Kiall stepped forward. 'I want to know about the sky pirates. You're the only person who has been inside a skyship and lived to tell the tale.'

'An imbecilic stunt that nearly cost me my life.'

'But it gave you the map that made your reputation and your fortune.'

'True, true.' Rad sat at his desk and gestured to a chair. 'Why do you want to know? Are you a minstrel planning a new heroic song?'

Kiall sat and cleared his throat a few times. 'No, I … I was just curious.'

'Listen, boy, there's no point in lying. If you

don't tell me truthfully why you want to know, I won't say another word.'

'I … it's a long story.'

'Oh, for — just spit it out!'

Kiall decided to reveal his family problems — it might make Rad feel sorry for him and then he'd get what he came for. He explained what had happened to his father and their suspicions of sabotage.

'Hmmm,' Rad said. 'It's not unheard of. Do you have a likely person in mind?'

'Not really. The main problem right now is that we have no money. Gold would pay the lawyer and the bribes.' As he saw Rad's face darken, he hastened on. 'I'm not asking for a loan. I plan to board a skyship and go back through a rift cave with them. Then I shall find gold and jewels aplenty to help my father.'

Rad burst out laughing, and kept guffawing for a full minute while Kiall's face turned a deep shade of red. Finally Rad wiped his eyes. 'That's the funniest thing I've heard in weeks.'

'I'm serious.'

'Sky pirates would eat a boy like you alive. After cutting you up into bite-sized pieces first. You wouldn't have a chance.'

'I'm no younger than you were when you went on their ship.'

'And no less stupid, by the sound of it.' Rad examined Kiall's face for several long seconds, then shrugged. 'All right, since I have nothing better to do today, I'll tell you what you want to know. But only because I know you won't make it off the rooftop.'

Kiall pressed his lips together to stop himself grinning like a circus clown. He nodded and waited.

'The skyships come at night. They have large hulls and black sails, and move as silently as ghosts. You have to look for dark patches in the sky and hope that a ladder is thrown down near you. The pirates climb down, steal whatever they can and leave. They carry scimitars so sharp they could trim your eyebrows with them and they move faster than gutter rats. Do you understand so far?'

'Yes.'

'They are the ugliest things I have ever seen come out of the rift caves from other worlds, and that includes the Zolka. Like skeletons covered in oiled parchment. And great yellow tusks. Ugh.'

'What is inside the ships?'

Rad shrugged. 'I don't really know.'

'But —'

'I was in the hold — where they store their stolen goods. What is above that is guesswork. It's where they fly the ship from, and where the magic metal thing is that powers it.'

'So I could hide behind their booty. Or carry a sack with me and hide inside that.' Kiall's brain ticked off the possibilities. 'And take some food in case I'm there for a while.'

'Oh, you'll be there for a while, all right. Because how are you going to get back?' Rad asked. 'If you get on an empty ship, there will be nowhere to hide, and who says it will return to Quentaris anyway? You might end up being sold as a slave in Lavaria, like me.'

'I'll find a way,' Kiall said stubbornly.

'No, you won't.' Rad stood, flicking his hand at Kiall. 'Go on, be off with you. It's a ridiculous and dangerous idea. Go home and help your mother. That will be of far more use to your family than this stupid sky pirate plan.'

Tears burned in Kiall's eyes, but he was determined not to let Rad see them. He left the office and charged down the stairs, pushing Wickle out of his way, ignoring the man's 'Hoy!' He ran along the street, turning away from the fork that led to his family's home and heading to the market. This morning he'd tucked the silver neck chain he'd received for his birthday into his pocket, thinking he could use it to help with his father's bail bond. Now there was no bail allowed, the chain would buy a serviceable dagger instead. That, along with his sack and some food and water, would be all he'd need on the skyship.

What did the pompous, dung-brained Rad de La'rel know anyway?

3
All
Aboard

KIALL SHIVERED IN THE cool night air and wished he was on a roof with a warm chimney to sit against, but this was an area of flat-roofed houses with chimneys behind the parapeted walls. He'd chosen it for two reasons — the people who lived here were wealthy and were likely targets for pirates. Also, they used their roofs for sitting outside when they dined, so there were doors into the houses below. And flat roofs were a

31

lot easier to run across when trying to grab hold of a rope ladder.

Kiall thought about trying to dodge sky pirates with skeletal faces to climb their ladder, and swallowed hard. His stomach churned so much that the aroma of meat cooking somewhere below had no effect on him at all. He wished the pirates would hurry up and arrive; waiting gave him too much time to brood on what might go wrong, and he refused to consider failure.

This was his third night of watching for sky pirates. Every day he had gone with his mother to visit his father and cringed at the shouting and moaning from those in the cells around him. The dungeons smelled of rotting flesh and mould, and the walls were green with slimy moss. After the visits, he'd had to lie to his mother and pretend he was out visiting friends and begging for money, but he couldn't bear the humiliation. She'd found a lawyer who promised to get Paolo released on bail, but not until she'd paid him twenty royals. So far she'd begged and borrowed five. Between his father's drawn face and his mother's tears every night, Kiall's resolve to board the skyship only grew stronger.

He sighed and fidgeted, trying to ease the ache in his rear end. Maybe he should have brought a cushion to sit on. For the hundredth time, he scanned the sky, remembering Rad's words. *You have to look for dark patches in the sky.*

Wait! Surely that was one out to his right? He jumped up and ran to the parapet, peering up. Yes, it was. It had to be. About two hundred yards away, moving slowly — no, it had stopped. There was movement below it. Pirates coming down the ladder. It was time to move. Before the person on watch rang the bell and scared them off.

Kiall grabbed his sack and climbed the parapet, running lightly across the narrow bridge to the next roof, and then the one after that. He'd spent hours up here, working out all the shortcuts the roof crawlers used to get around and using them until he knew them off by heart. Several times maids and servants had caught him, but he'd lied and pretended to be a roofie.

There was the ladder, swinging in the breeze, one roof over. He leaped across the last small gap and landed on the roof. What was that? A noise behind him. He glanced around, but saw nothing. The pirates must be in the house below. Maybe he heard them dropping something. There was no time to lose. Rad said they moved quickly, so he had to stay ahead of them. He hooked the sack over his shoulder, grasped a rung of the ladder above him and began climbing.

It was a long way up and his arms and legs began to burn with the effort, but he kept going, hand over hand, one foot up, then the other. Twice he looked up to make sure there wasn't a pirate waiting at the top for him, but the way was clear. At last he reached the top and crawled through the trapdoor in the bottom of the ship. Gasping for breath, he lay flat on the decking. A rattle from the ladder sent him staggering, searching for a place to hide before the pirates returned and caught him.

As Rad had warned, there were no convenient stacks of boxes and chests. There were just a few piles of silver and gold plates, candelabra, cloth and furs. Kiall examined the plates and candelabra — would they fetch enough at the market to pay for his father's lawyer? Probably. But it wasn't enough. Kiall knew that what he really wanted was a large bag of gold and jewels, worth enough not only to free his father but to finance a new business so huge and successful that they would have more power than scum like Tash Morley. He also wanted enough money to pay Quentaris's finest investigators to find out who the saboteurs were, and crush them to dust.

So he would forge ahead with his plan, find the wealth he desired so badly, and then return victorious. But right now, he had to find somewhere to hide.

He could hear loud rattling behind him. The pirates were returning and he had to move fast. He scooted behind the largest pile of plates and pulled two thick furs over himself, huddling down into a small ball. The fur was dank and musty, and its odour coated the inside of his nose and throat like fuzz. He badly wanted to cough but managed to stifle it.

Where were the pirates? Were they all back on board? A strange whistling sound began and then the deck beneath him pitched sharply sideways. He slid back and then forward again, clutching the fur tightly around him. Something banged into him and he squawked, then cursed himself for making a noise, but no one hauled the fur off him and shouted the alarm.

A loud clatter scared him so greatly that he bit his tongue. He shrank down even further, tasting the iron blood in his mouth. After a few minutes, nothing more happened and he relaxed a little. That sound must have been the pirates throwing more booty on the pile. The deck pitched and lurched again and he decided that the ship was definitely moving faster. It must be heading back to the rift caves.

This was it. He was on his way. How long would it take? Rift adventurers who travelled on foot were gone for days or weeks but he wasn't sure how much faster the skyship was, or how long the adventurers spent trading or stealing treasures from other worlds. He felt for the water bottle and packet of bread and cheese in his sack. No, wait a while longer before pushing the fur aside. Too risky yet.

Something poked him in the leg and then knocked against his head. He froze. Was a pirate stabbing through the furs with a pike?

'Kiall! Kiall! You can come out now. They've gone up to the top deck.'

Huh? Was that ...? It couldn't be. But it was. Maya. Kiall threw the fur off and stared at his sister. She was dressed all in black, her long hair tightly braided, her face covered in some kind of dark paint. 'What are you doing here?' He wanted to strangle her. How dare she ruin his plan!

'I've come along to save you,' she said, grinning, her teeth white in her blackened face.

'I don't need saving,' he spluttered. 'Go back. You'll ruin everything.'

'Of course I won't. You can't do this alone. You need some brains with you.'

'I am perfectly intelligent!'

'Yes, but also impulsive. Have you thought, for example, about what you will do at the other end?'

'Ye-es.' His chin jutted out. 'Well, no, but I wager that neither have you.'

'I don't know what we'll find.'

'Aha! See?'

'But I have a plan. They'll be unloading all of this, ready to trade or sell it.' She pointed to the other end of the storage deck. It was in total darkness. 'I have two black silk sheets. If we hide in the farthest corner with the sheets over us, they'll never see us. We'll wait until they've unloaded and left the ship, then we'll sneak out. Well? What do you think?'

'I suppose that might work,' he said grudgingly.

'Might? It's better than anything you've thought of. Which is nothing.'

'I would have, by the time I got there,' Kiall said. 'Did you bring any food? I have bread and cheese.'

'Yuck. I have chicken legs and cinnamon cake.' Maya opened her bag and pulled out the wrapped packets.

'I thought we were too poor now for food like that,' Kiall said, his mouth watering at the smell.

'Might be the last decent food we have for a while,' she said. 'Save your food for when we're desperate.'

After eating, they lay down on the furs to rest, but stayed ready to hide if there were any signs of the pirates coming to check down below. When the whistling noise had grown louder with a slight echo, they decided the ship must be in a rift cave. Soon after, they passed through something that made the inside of the hold glow faintly green. 'That must be the rift,' Maya said. 'No going back now.'

Kiall felt a cold finger trail down his spine. No going back. How long would it take to reach the pirates' world? He'd heard stories of how the rift caves worked, and how time seemed to move differently, depending on where you were and where the caves led. He thought Maya's idea to use the sheets was good, but if they arrived in bright daylight, surely they'd be seen?

His eyelids drooped and although he fought to stay awake, sleep battered down his defences and took him away.

Maya shook him awake. 'Hurry! We're there. Take this sheet.'

She hauled him to his feet and they ran to the other end of the hold, trying to tread lightly. The whistling had stopped — now he could hear thumping above and shouting outside. It was still dark, thank the gods, and he joined Maya in the prow of the ship, throwing the sheet around himself and squashing in next to her against the bulkhead.

'Crouch down,' Maya hissed. 'Make sure all of you is covered.'

He caught sight of a pair of boots descending the runged ladder in the mid-section. For once, he obeyed her without arguing. It was agony, not being able to see where the pirates were, but all the stowaways could do was stay still and silent. Soon, however, Kiall's legs began to cramp from crouching. 'I have to sit,' he whispered frantically, 'or I'll fall over.'

'Wait.'

He felt Maya shift slightly and realised she was peering out from under her sheet. Her blackened face would be less noticeable. After many long, painful seconds, she whispered, 'Sit now. Quickly.'

He managed to change position and gradually the cramps eased, leaving him soaked in sweat. At the other end of the hold, there were a lot of loud crashes and foul curses before all activity finally ceased.

Maya moved a little and then said, 'They've all gone. So has the booty. And I think the sun has risen.'

Kiall pulled the sheet from his face, sucking in long breaths of cool air, and then uncoiled himself and tried to stand. He felt as if his legs were rusty hinges. 'What now?' he asked.

'I'm going to have a look at what's outside, and then we'll need a plan.'

'Another one?'

Maya scowled at him and walked over to the trapdoor. She opened it a few inches, knelt down and peered out. Kiall eyed the ladder leading upwards. He could see that there was nothing to be gained in going up there, especially if a pirate had been left on guard.

Maya stood, frowning. 'I can't see anything. We seem to be resting on the ground.'

'Huh?' Kiall looked through the trapdoor. There was only solid rock beneath them. 'How did they get their booty out then?'

'There must be another door in the side of the ship.' Maya began inspecting the hull near the trapdoor. 'I think they were over here somewhere.'

Kiall walked further along, running his hands over the hull, trying to find a door and noticing pinpoints of light here and there. A strange keening sound caught his attention. It started as a whine, dipped into a strange growl and then slid up to a high-pitched howl. The hairs on his head stood straight and he stepped back from the hull. 'What in the heavens is *that*?'

Maya shook her head. 'I have no idea. I think it's outside. Is it —'

In front of them, the side of the ship fell away and a bright light speared them to the floor. Kiall was blinded and flung his hands over his eyes, stumbling backwards. He felt something heavy and furry brush past his leg, once, twice, and then a bitter, choking smell filled his nose and throat.

'Ah, extra cargo,' a rasping voice said. 'How nice.'

4
Captured

THE SEARING SUNLIGHT KEPT Kiall and Maya blinded as rough hands took hold of them and Kiall's dagger was lifted from his belt. Their captors shoved the twins together, tied their arms behind their backs and pulled them towards the door of the ship.

Kiall tripped on the sill of the door and one of his captors jerked him upright. 'He's a derfus, this one. Never sell 'im.'

'I think they'd bring a fairly pocket full as a matchin' pair,' another said. 'Or I'd buy this un for her pretty face.'

Kiall bristled and tried to yank his arms free, but the rope cut into his wrists. He blinked and focused on the men nearest him. To his surprise, these were not the skeletal sky pirates, but they were pirates nonetheless. Their faces were scarred, their skin weathered and lined, and their arms were tattooed with strange creatures. A tall man in a dark purple coat stepped in front of Kiall and slapped the side of his head. The blow rocked Kiall back and made his ears ring.

'No use fighting,' the man rasped. 'There's nowhere to run. Take a look around.'

For the first time, Kiall looked past his captors, out at the blasted landscape. He shuddered. In the harsh light he saw an endless dust-blown red plain, so barren it was as if forty fire and earth magicians had battled for days until all that was left was dead earth. There wasn't even a horizon — just a blur-ring in the distance. He thought he could see some cracks across the surface here and there, but the heat shimmer made it hard to be sure. As he watched, a small dust storm blew up in the east and travelled quickly across the plain before dying down again.

Behind the ship was a row of low red mountains with several deep fissures cut into their bases. In these sat another skyship, and a normal ship with three masts and rows of reefed sails. What was that doing here? There was no water in sight. Then Kiall saw the wheels attached to the hull.

'Take them to the *Shiba* and lock them in the brig,' the man rasped.

'They not going to de slave market?' one of the pirates asked.

'I need crew now. I can't wait for the bartering at the market.' The man shrugged off his coat and shirt, revealing tattooed skin underneath. A picture of a sinuous striped cat flowed across his chest, its tail curling around his arm. The weird growling began again. A cat appeared and padded softly towards its master as if it recognised itself on his skin. The cat was as big as a hunting dog, with gold stripes across its dark brown fur, and two gleaming sabre teeth that curved down past its jaw. As it padded past Kiall, its feral smell singed his nose and he gagged.

'Shift yourselves along!' the man snapped. 'Sun is higher.'

Sure enough, the huge red ball was surging up from the east and already its heat baked their skins. The pirates hauled Kiall and Maya across the stony ground to the sailing ship and forced them to climb the wooden ladder on its side. As they reached the deck, a boy, smaller than Kiall, with fair, shaggy hair, started striking a large metal bell with a hammer. 'Captain Blackwine coming aboard!' he shouted. 'Stand at attention, you dogs.'

There was no one else on the deck, but the pirates holding Kiall and Maya snapped to attention and saluted as the man jumped lightly from the rail to the deck and saluted them back. He tossed his coat and shirt to the boy and headed for an oaken door, opening it and disappearing from sight.

''Ere, Davin.' The pirate next to Kiall shoved him towards the boy. ''Ese two go in brig for now. Make sure 'ee lock 'em up good.'

Another peered at Maya's face. 'This be paint. Wash her off.'

Davin sighed. 'Can they sail? Who's going to train them?'

'You, a course! An' if you don' do a good job, we're eating 'em.' The pirates laughed and slapped each other's backs so it was hard to tell if they were serious, but Kiall felt sick.

They went below, leaving Kiall and Maya with the boy, who inspected them with great interest once they were alone. 'Where did you come from?'

'Quentaris,' Kiall said.

'Ooohhh,' Davin said. 'And you came *here*?'

Kiall and Maya glanced at each other and Maya shook her head. It was better not to say anything.

Kiall didn't want to think about how they would ever return, let alone with the treasure he'd dreamed of. What a joke.

'What is this land?' Maya asked. 'It is so bare and … horrible.'

'Selinium,' Davin said. 'The old stories say it didn't used to be like this.' He shrugged. 'Who knows? Come on, I have to lock you up, but once we set sail, you'll be out.'

Davin led them down two sets of wooden steps, into the dark, smelly hold. They passed the galley where a tiny man laboured over a fire in a brick oven and half a dozen pirates sat at a table, tearing into whole roast birds. In the hold, Davin opened a small door and pointed inside. 'You have to go in there.'

'Can you untie us first?' Maya asked. 'It's hard to

sit down when your arms are bound.'

'I suppose so. You won't get past the crew so don't bother to try and escape.' He pulled at the sailor's knots and the ropes loosened. 'I'll bring you some food.'

Kiall's stomach grumbled at the thought of roast chicken. It had been a long time since their last meal. They settled on the floor, half-falling against each other and then leaning against the bulwark. 'If this ship goes out on that huge plain, how will we escape?' Maya said. 'Let alone get back to the rift cave.'

'At least we're not being shipped off to the slave market,' Kiall said. 'I'm sure things will work out.' Even as he said the words, he didn't believe them. They were in deep trouble, and they might as well be slaves if they were prisoners on this ship and expected to work to stay alive.

A few minutes later, Davin brought back a wooden platter that held some pieces of what look-ed like chicken and two hunks of dry bread. 'This is all that's left,' he said, 'and there's no water to spare. You'll have to drink murgo.' He put a metal bottle and a filthy cloth next to the platter.

'Thanks,' Maya said. When he'd locked the door

again and left, they grabbed a piece of the meat each. 'It smells funny,' she said. 'Do you think it's poisoned?'

'No, but it's not chicken.' Kiall sniffed the meat. 'Some kind of bird — it's just gamey, I hope.' He took a bite and chewed. 'Strong, but it's all right.'

'Have you still got your waterskin?'

'No, it's on the skyship.'

Maya sipped from the bottle and coughed. 'Eergh. This is like the spirits old Jasto next door distils from corn and mash. We'd be drunk in a minute if we drank it.' She poured some on the cloth and wiped her face clean. 'It makes good soap.'

'I wonder where they get water from then. This land is all desert. But they can't drink that stuff all the time.'

Before Maya could answer, there was a lot of shouting and thumping above them and the ship lurched, then it began to move. They could hear a rattling rumble beneath them and more shouting.

'The wheels are turning. We're going … somewhere,' Kiall said.

The door to their prison swung open and Davin beckoned. 'Come on, the rope team is pulling us out to the wind gap. You're wanted on the sails.'

Kiall shoved the last piece of meat in his mouth and some bread into his pocket. Maya did the same, and they followed Davin back up to the top deck. All around them, the ship groaned and creaked as if it was about to fall apart with the strain. By the time they got to the main mast, the rope team was coiling up two huge lines and climbing back on board. The ship was at the edge of the plain, directly in line with a gap between two mountains. From behind them a wind whistled down and rattled the lines and sail fastenings.

Davin pointed upwards. 'You two have to get up there and lower the sails. You'd better hurry — Captain Blackwine wants to get to Grave Valley before midday.'

'But —' Maya looked for a ladder of some kind.

'Over there,' Davin said, pushing her one way and Kiall the other. 'Up the ratlines.'

The ratlines were a flimsy web of ropes strung from each side of the ship up to the top of the first yardarm. From there, another web stretched higher. When still they hesitated, Davin picked up a pike with a viciously sharp spearhead and hook on one end and thrust it forward. 'You'll get this in your back if you don't get up there now.'

'Do as he says,' Blackwine growled. He stood by the wheel on the rear deck, watching. 'Or I'll add my cutlass.'

As Kiall and Maya climbed onto the webs, Davin shouted, 'Untie the lower sail first, then go up to the next. And don't forget to hang on tight!'

Kiall needed no instruction about hanging on. As soon as he left the deck, the wind ripped at his clothes and whipped him around on the ratlines. He lost his footing, dangling awkwardly until he could pull himself up and keep climbing, learning quickly to grasp the ropes securely with his hands before moving his feet.

Across the other side, Maya was faring no better, her face deathly white, her eyes closed as she moved by touch alone.

Kiall reached the yardarm before Maya did and waited until she was next to him. The wind battered at them as if trying to push them off and fling them out onto the hard red dirt.

'We'll have to do this together,' Kiall said, 'or one of us will be knocked off. I'll count.'

'You'll have to shout,' Maya said, 'or I won't hear you further out.'

'All right. Now look,' he said, pointing, 'these are

like the ones on Papa's ships. Pull this end and the knot will come loose. Ready?'

Maya nodded and Kiall said, 'First one, now!' They each pulled a tie loose and stepped along the rope to the next one. 'Second, now!' Three more steps. 'Third, now!' The wind yanked at the sail as it began to unfurl, making it flap wildly and ram up against their feet. Two ties to go, then one. The sail filled with wind and tightened to bursting. The rope their feet rested on bounced up and down. Now they had to get back to the mast. He looked down at the deck. Davin gazed up, his face twisted, but Blackwine was yelling at the pirates to belay the lines. The ship moved forward slowly.

Davin gestured up at them. 'Get the next one! Hurry!'

Kiall couldn't afford to check where Maya was. Every ounce of his concentration was focused on keeping his feet on the rope and his hands clutching the yardarm so he wouldn't fall. By the time he neared the mast, Blackwine was below him on the deck.

'Get up to the next sail now, or you'll feel hot lead,' the captain ordered. He brandished a strange-looking stick, then aimed it at Kiall.

The stick jerked and banged, and wood splinters flew out of the mast near Kiall's head. He could see a long gouge in the wood. Whatever that was, if the next one hit him, he would certainly die.

He yelled, 'Maya, go up! Follow me,' and began climbing into the next ratline webbing.

'I'm up here,' she shouted back, and he caught sight of her feet above him.

At the next yardarm, she said, 'We did that the wrong way. We have to start at the end and work in.'

Of course. Why hadn't he realised that? He edged outwards, following her lead, fighting to keep hold of the yardarm. The wind was so strong now that it seared his skin and snapped the sails away from the ties within a split second of him loosening them. At least this time he was heading in towards the mast instead of facing that torturous trip back. He refused to think about going down, but of course they had to. Compared to the footline, the webbing was a haven of safety. When he stepped down at last onto the solid deck, his legs buckled underneath him and he fell heavily.

A boot landed against his ribs, hard enough to hurt but not break anything. 'Get up,' Davin commanded. 'You're not finished yet. You have to raise the foresails.'

'More climbing?' Kiall asked, staggering to his feet.

'Pulling on ropes, with those two.'

Davin prodded Kiall forward to join two pirates hauling on a thick rope that raised a smaller sail inch by inch. On the other side, Maya helped two more pirates; their combined strength made her look like an elf on the end of the rope.

'Belay the line, girl,' one growled. 'Yer no good for else.' She did what he said and wound the rope once around a wooden double handle, keeping the rope taut as the sail went up, then winding it four times more to fix it at the end. Kiall did the same on his side, his hands burning. Now the ship moved at a faster rate, its wheels rumbling loudly and its planks and decking creaking. He glanced over the rail and saw Blackwine's huge cat running easily next to the ship like a silent sentinel. It clearly wasn't the kind of pet that curled up on cushions.

Kiall's mouth was bone-dry and his throat ached. The pirates drank deeply from their bottles and he wondered if they had water or spirits. One near him belched loudly and the fumes from his mouth answered the question. Maybe they were used to it, but Kiall craved a small cup of water more than he had ever wanted anything in his life.

Maya joined him at the rail. 'Now what?'

'You can rest for a while,' Davin said. He stood up near the bow, holding a compass and scanning the land ahead. 'In about twenty minutes, we'll be tacking and you'll be back on the ropes.'

'Can we have some water?' Kiall asked.

Davin shook his head. 'Not until we reach Grave Valley. We have none left.'

Kiall sank down against the bulwark. 'Where are you going to find a valley out here?'

'You'll see when we get there,' Davin said as he walked past them. 'Be ready when you're called. Captain likes the idea of using you as target practice for his pistol.'

Maya sank down beside Kiall. 'What does he mean — target?'

'Didn't you see him with that stick? It made a big hole in the mast.'

'What stick would do that?'

'Don't know. Davin called it a pistol. It's like nothing I've ever seen. But I don't want him using it on me again.'

The sun was a quarter of the way up the sky now, and had changed from warming to burning. Blackwine and the pirates had all donned large brimmed hats, and Davin brought two over to Kiall and Maya.

'You'll need to wear these now until sunset,' he said. 'Otherwise the sun will make you very sick.'

They nodded and put the hats on, immediately feeling the burning heat fade. It was hot enough sitting — working on the ropes would be unbearable, but they'd have no choice. Blackwine needed them as crew, but it seemed he was just as happy to kill them for sport. Kiall wanted to cry over how badly his plan had turned out, but what would Maya think? They only had each other now for support. Papa in prison was part of another world, one so far away it was as if it no longer existed. Was he even now wondering where they were? Why they hadn't visited him?

For the first time, Kiall saw that Rad had been right. Chasing sky pirates was a stupid thing to do. They should both be in Quentaris helping their mother. He had failed his father, failed his whole family. Black despair swept over him and he bowed his head, wishing that the yardarm would fall and knock him unconscious so he wouldn't have to bear this shame any longer.

Maya poked him. 'Stop it!'

'What?'

'You're giving up, I can tell. Stop it right now.'

'I'm not!' He sat up straighter, took a deep breath. They were still alive. There was still hope.

5
Attack!

A SHOUT WENT UP and Kiall and Maya were sent back to the ropes again. The wind that had been pushing the ship along at high speed was noticeably dying, and they slowed to walking pace.

Kiall let go of his rope and the pirate in front of him barked, 'Hold dat rope. She is changing quick.' Kiall just had time to grab the rope again when a gust burst in from starboard.

'Bring her around!' Blackwine shouted. 'Hold those ropes!' The ship heeled sharply. The sails banged and snapped and Kiall could feel the wheels on his side lift off the ground. The pirates from Maya's side pounded across the deck and leaned over the rail until the ship steadied, then ran back to their rope. The wind increased and they were off again, surging forward then falling back a little. Davin and another pirate ran to the stern to tighten the small rudder sail.

The wind from this direction wasn't as constant, and there was much letting out of sailcloth and pulling in again to make the most of each gust. Kiall and Maya were run off their feet, yelled at from all directions and cuffed hard several times for not being fast enough to follow orders. It was obvious that they needed another half dozen crew to cope with the changing conditions, but those on deck had to manage as best they could.

Finally they were told to stand fast and wait, and Davin had his compass out again, directing the man angling the rudder sail. Blackwine stood near the bow, staring out, apparently waiting for something. Kiall realised he was watching the cat, which had run ahead of them and was casting around, tail held high. Then it turned and howled, its voice faint beyond the ship's din, and Blackwine shouted, 'There! Ten degrees to the west.'

Davin shouted back to the rudderman and the ship turned slightly, heading towards what looked like a huge crevasse. At the last minute, they sailed down into a long dip instead. Two pirates ran nimbly up the ratlines to reef in the mainsail, and Kiall and Maya were sent back to help wind out two large triple-hooked anchors from the capstan. Gradually the ship slowed, gliding between rows of tree stumps and, as the anchors bit deep and stopped the ship completely, two more pirates leapt overboard.

'Get those ropes out!' Davin shouted at Kiall and Maya, pointing to the coils near the rear deck. They each hauled a coil to the rail and threw it over to the pirates waiting below who tied the ropes to the stumps. After hours of thumping and rattling across the plain, the silence that fell now was like being deep inside a cave.

Kiall tried to lick his dry lips but he had not a drop of saliva in his mouth. He leant against the rail, feeling faint, but there was no time for resting.

'Help with the barrels,' Davin said. 'We roll them down the poles and then tie them up.'

Together, the twins carried four large empty barrels up from the hold and rolled them down the parallel poles. At the bottom, the pirates caught them and tied them onto lighter poles for carrying. The cat stayed in the shade under the ship but its odour drifted up on the breeze. When all the barrels were ready, Kiall was put on the front end of two poles and Maya on the rear, like the other pirates. Blackwine and Davin, carrying leather bags, headed the procession. They all set off towards the edge of the crevasse.

'Maybe there's a river at the bottom,' Kiall said, but he doubted it. The land here was solid rock and their boots echoed as they walked.

Yet when they reached a wide path cut into the rock and began to walk down a steep slope, he saw he was right. Twenty yards below the edge, pale green and white shrubs grew. As they descended, the undergrowth became greener and more lush. They turned a sharp corner and began climbing down a set of carved steps. The valley opened out before them. It was filled with leafy trees and a silver thread of water wound across the floor. Small groups of houses sat on rises above the water and Kiall was astonished to see people gathered in the clearings, waving and calling greetings.

Maya laughed behind him. 'First time I've ever seen anyone pleased to spy pirates on the horizon.'

Davin, who had waited for them at the bottom of the steps, said, 'Here we are traders.'

'They believe that?' Kiall said.

'Why not? We do them no harm.'

Kiall frowned. This didn't make sense, but he kept quiet, waiting to see what would happen. The villagers of the valley greeted them happily, carrying out huge trays of food and drink, and a celebration followed. Kiall and Maya were given fresh water to drink and invited to eat whatever they wanted. Most of the food consisted of fish dishes and vegetables, light and delicious, and they ate until their stomachs were full to bursting. The villagers were all small and very dark, dressed in colourful shifts and pants of a light material. They appeared to be used to the heat and dressed to suit the climate. They also ate little, drinking mostly water or fruit juice, waiting for the visitors to finish.

Then came the trading. Davin and Blackwine opened their leather bags and tipped out the contents onto woven mats. Jewels of every hue, and gold and silver necklaces and bracelets spilled out in a sparkling rainbow. The chief of the villagers, a stocky man with a huge ruby on a thick gold chain around his neck, knelt by the mat and inspected the offerings. Then he beckoned to three others who took over, sorting and counting, weighing and measuring, recording their results with marks on sheets of bleached matting.

Blackwine waited patiently, fanning himself with a large leaf, the tattooed cat on his chest seeming to breathe as he fanned. At last the chief was satisfied with the tallying and began an earnest conversation with Blackwine, who appeared to speak their language with ease. There was a great deal of nodding and various 'Oha!' noises and, after final handclasps, a group of villagers left and returned with more than a dozen bolts of cloth.

As each one was partially unravelled, Kiall marvelled at the brilliant colours. Maya nudged him. 'Look closer — the cloth has gold and jewels woven into it. It's amazing. I've never seen anything like it.'

Davin leant their way. 'These people are the only craftsmen capable of such work. Fair trading is the only means we have to get this cloth.'

That explained a lot. Rampaging pirates might

get the first bolts of cloth by stealing it, but they would also be the last. A bit like ripping up the whole plant to get valuable healing balm from it, but it would never grow again.

'What about the barrels?' Maya asked.

'Yes,' Davin said, smiling, 'we also barter for water.'

Thank the gods! No doubt they would soon be back out on the plain and the thought of all those barrels of water on the ship made it easier to bear.

After filling the barrels and tying them back on the poles, it was time to trudge back to the ship. Blackwine evidently had no desire to stay overnight in the village. The trip up the rock steps took forever, and Kiall and Maya both stumbled and fell several times, grazing their knees and receiving grumbled threats from Blackwine. He was in a good mood after the trading, however, and didn't actually beat them for their slow progress.

The pirates hauled the barrels up onto the ship, as the twins weren't able to manage such loads, but they were both put on the ropes. The ship had to be manually pulled up out of the dip, the whole crew working like packhorses, until the wind caught the sails again. They didn't travel far, just to a low ridge a bit further west, where the sails were lowered again and one anchor hammered into the rock.

'Why are we staying here?' Kiall asked Davin.

'Now we are pirates again,' was all he would say.

They were allowed to sleep but had to stay on the deck, ready to work if required. Kiall lay back, watching the small silver moon rise like a balloon and sit high in the sky. It gave off a constant pale light, unlike the full moon in Quentaris that created dark shadows under eaves and along walls. What was Papa doing right now? Probably still in prison. Although it felt like he and Maya had been with the pirates for weeks, it was really only about two days. Mama would be scouring the streets for them, worried sick.

Maya yawned beside him. 'I wonder what Mama is doing?' she whispered.

'Threatening to beat us black and blue,' Kiall said. 'If she ever finds us. Which she won't.'

'We shouldn't have left her on her own.' Maya's voice was quiet. Kiall turned towards her.

'And now we're slaves and probably will never get back to Quentaris. What will Papa think of us?'

'At least we tried to do something. We could have done nothing to help her. Who do we know with money to lend?' Maya brightened. 'This may be foolhardy, but just think — one bolt of that cloth and our fortunes are made!'

'Now you're starting to sound like me,' Kiall teased.

'We have always been a team,' Maya said. 'Remember how we used to steal pastries off Mistress Boon's stall? I'd cry my eyes out and you'd take a handful when she was comforting me.'

Kiall grinned. 'They were the best pastries in the market.'

'This is no different. All we have to do is be ready to take our chance. Blackwine will return to the rift cave sooner or later. Where else would he sell this cloth except in other lands or cities like Quentaris?'

'So you're telling me to be patient,' Kiall said.

'I know that is almost impossible for you,' Maya said. 'But yes, patience is our best weapon.'

Having reached agreement of sorts on what to do next, they both drifted off to uncomfortable sleep on the hard deck.

They were woken by the cat's howl, low and menacing. Kiall jerked upright and found Davin next to him.

'Sshh,' Davin whispered. 'A ship is coming. You'll get the signal soon to man the sails.'

'How far away is it?' Kiall said softly.

'A while yet. Sly senses them through the earth before she smells them.'

'Sly?'

'The cat. You don't think Captain keeps her just as a pet, do you? Everyone works on this ship.' His tone was bitter, and Kiall wondered for the first time if Davin was here by choice, or by circumstance, like them.

'What are we going to do with this ship?'

'Attack it, of course.' Davin lay down again. 'No hurry. Portus will stir us when it's time.' He stared up into the black sky for a few seconds. 'Is Quentaris as wonderful as they say?'

Kiall snorted. 'Depends who you are. If you have money and power, yes.'

'Is your family poor?'

'They weren't, until someone sabotaged us.' Kiall sighed. 'It's a long story. But yes, Quentaris is a wonderful city, full of life and music and exciting people from strange worlds.'

'It is my dream to go there,' Davin whispered. 'To live there. I hate this arid place with its heat and red dirt, and people living in holes in the ground.'

'Are you a slave then?' Kiall asked. 'You're stuck here, like us?'

'Not really. Well, stuck in a different way.'

'Stir 'ee!' a voice hissed out of the darkness. 'Up to sails.'

'That's you,' Davin said. 'I'm on the cannon.'

Kiall was given no time to ask questions. Within seconds, he and Maya were once again climbing the ratlines, using touch to find the ropes as the darkness was complete now the moon had gone. Without speaking, they met at the mast and each edged out to the end of the main yardarm, ready to undo the ties. There was barely a sound from below, just some scuffling and whispered commands, then a scraping that Kiall guessed was the anchor being dragged in and roped up.

Several long minutes passed, then there was another hissed command to let out the sails. The mainsail dropped and they headed up for the next one. The *Shiba* moved slowly forward, past the rocky outcrop and onto the flat plain. The wind was now blowing from the east — were the wind patterns constant or ever-changing? How could anyone get where they needed to go without knowing when and where each wind would drive them? Was it so different at sea?

Night was coming to an end. Far away to the east, a ruddy glow tiptoed across the plain and gradually Kiall could make out the shape of their ship, and then the pirates standing at the rails, holding short swords and pikes. He wondered where Davin was, then saw him in the bow with a strange, thick metal tube, nearly the length of his leg, mounted on a trolley. Next to him was a box of large iron balls.

The *Shiba* was moving faster now as the wind picked up, heading north, and from his vantage point up the mast Kiall saw another ship moving quickly on a path diagonal to them. If the *Shiba* sped up, the two ships would meet in about half a mile; otherwise, the other ship would get away. As if reading his thoughts, the pirates downed weapons to raise the foresails and the *Shiba* rushed forward.

'Get down!' Davin shouted to the twins. They scrambled to the deck, and Kiall went forward to see what Davin was doing. He was tipping black powder into the top of the tube.

'What is that?' Kiall asked.

'A cannon. Blackwine traded it from another rift world.' Davin pushed an iron ball into the tube. 'No one else has one. It makes them all easy pickings.'

There was no time to ask more questions. Davin ordered Maya to help him with the balls and Kiall to pick up the short curved sword at his feet.

Kiall hesitated — did they really expect him to fight like a pirate?

Obviously, yes. The pirate beside him said, ''Ee don't fight, 'ee get head chop off.' He grinned, his blackened teeth like mossy grave stones.

They were close enough now to the other ship to see her sailors running back and forth, pulling on ropes to get every inch of speed out of her and arming themselves with swords and staffs. There were many more of them than the pirates. How could the *Shiba* crew possibly defeat them?

Davin swivelled his strange tube in their direction. He touched a burning brand to the top and it exploded with an enormous bang and a cloud of smoke. On the other ship, a large hole appeared in its side and men screamed. Davin tipped in more black powder and Maya shoved a ball after it, then he touched the brand to the top again. Another explosion, and this time the main mast on the other ship toppled sideways, pulling sails and ropes with it, creating a huge mess on the deck and covering half of the sailors.

Kiall marvelled at the cannon. What an amazing weapon! So small and yet so lethal. From the other ship, a white flag shook vigorously in surrender. Blackwine steered the *Shiba* in close, the pirates throwing hooks across and pulling the ropes in so he could use his victim's crippled state to slow them both down.

Kiall and Maya were sent to reef the mainsails again, and by now they were getting quite skilled at it. From the yardarm, they watched as Blackwine leapt across the rails onto the other deck and raced to the wheel where the captain stood, holding the white flag. The man cowered back, begging for mercy, but Blackwine slashed down across his neck with his cutlass, then raised the severed head high. Blood splattered across his chest, dotting the tattooed cat, and dripped down his arms.

Maya gagged. 'What did he do that for? The man had surrendered!'

Kiall couldn't speak. The familiar vile smell seared his nostrils and he saw the cat run up to the ship, saliva drooling from its teeth as it waited for its reward. Blackwine tossed the head into the air. It landed on the ground and bounced once before the cat seized it in its jaws and ran off. Meanwhile, the pirates herded the sailors together and forced them to climb down off their ship. Not one protested.

'At least they won't drown, not like at sea,' Kiall said.

'No, out here they'll likely die of thirst and heat,' said Maya. 'They'll have to fix their mast before they can move again. That's if Captain Foul doesn't leap down and murder them all!'

The twins were ordered to help carry the plunder from the other ship, and Blackwine stood at the rail, inspecting each load. He discarded items such as furniture and clothing, only selecting things of value such as jewellery and ornate gewgaws that rich people might take a fancy to at the market. He had a keen eye for such things, and could tell in an instant what was real gold or silver and what was painted gilt.

Kiall kept his eyes down and followed every order, feeling like a snivelling coward, but after seeing what Blackwine was capable of, there was no point making him angry. Either of the twins' heads could be next to hit the ground.

Finally the ship was stripped of its valuables and left to wallow, broken-masted. Its crew stood some way off, huddled together, waiting for Blackwine to leave. Kiall hoped that they would give what was left of their captain a decent burial, although how they would make a hole in the rocky ground, he didn't know. From nowhere, a buzzing mass of large, black flies had settled on the corpse and, in the midday heat, the pool of blood had already dried dark brown.

The wind had died and the *Shiba*'s progress away from the plundered ship was slow. It was a relief to work the sails at a snail's pace instead of the frantic climbing and rope-pulling. Kiall had hoped they would head back to the mountains and the rift cave, but instead Blackwine set a course further south.

Maya went below to fill their water bottles and joined Kiall near the bow where he was trying to tie a length of cloth around his neck to stay cool. 'Here, let me do that,' she said, deftly folding the cloth into a triangle and knotting it. 'Where do you think we're going next?'

Kiall shrugged. 'More trading? Another valley?'

'That's right,' Davin said behind them. 'At this time of the year, when the winds aren't so strong, we stay out on the plain as long as possible.'

'What's it like when the winds really blow then?' Maya asked.

'Too rough for sailing,' Davin said. 'That's when we trade through the caves.'

'And plunder as well,' Kiall said.

Now it was Davin's turn to shrug. 'It's our life. Or rather it's Blackwine's.'

'You don't have to stay with him, do you?' Kiall asked. 'If you go to other lands, surely you could sneak away — choose somewhere he doesn't go very often.'

'It's not that simple,' Davin said. He checked the level of the sun above them and the mast's shadow across the deck. 'The afternoon squalls will come soon, so be ready.'

'Again?' Kiall groaned.

'The life of a sailor,' Davin said, and laughed rather unkindly.

The squalls were not as bad as Kiall expected, and lasted only until dusk; the plain fell into silent darkness and when the sails were reefed and the anchor out, they were allowed to eat. The spoils from the other ship included a side of meat that looked like goat, freshly killed. It had been cooking slowly all afternoon on a spit in the galley. Everyone's mouth was watering at the aroma — Kiall was ready to steal a portion, he was so hungry. At last the meat was divided up between them all and they sat on the deck, ripping into the charred flesh, juices dripping from their chins. Blackwine deigned to eat with them, chewing silently, then took two choice cuts of the meat to feed to his cat. Kiall and Maya were allowed to sleep below with the pirates, but found the snoring and stench overwhelming so went back to the open air on the deck.

'What are we going to do?' Maya said, when they'd lain down. 'We could be out here for months, killing people or, more likely, getting killed ourselves. Blackwine is a murderer.'

'Er, he's a pirate,' Kiall reminded her. 'But you're right. We have to find a way to make Blackwine head back to the rift cave.'

'He's on a trading and piracy route here. He won't be easily diverted.' She frowned. 'Unless something happens to this ship.'

'We can't wreck it. We'll never get back. We can't mutiny — the other pirates won't help us. And Davin won't either.'

'What about ...' Maya tapped her fingers against

her lips. 'This is a very wide plain, wider than any around Quentaris. If Blackwine is planning on travelling to the other side, he'll need a ship that can cope with these horrible winds.'

'Yes. So?'

Maya checked around them to make sure no one had come on deck without being noticed. She lowered her voice to a faint whisper all the same. 'If the mainsail was damaged, the ship could still sail but not properly. I'm sure there are no spares below. He'd have to go back and get another sail from a skyship.'

Kiall rolled over and hugged her. 'You are brilliant!'

'Well, yes,' she said, laughing. 'But it won't be easy. We don't have a knife or a cutlass, except the ones Blackwine gives us for an attack. We'll have to wait and watch, take our chance when it comes.'

'I'm ready.'

'Ready for sleep. Who knows where we'll be this time tomorrow?'

'Heading back to Quentaris,' Kiall said, 'if I've got anything to do with it.'

6
Secret
Allies

THE NEXT MORNING, EVERYONE rose early. Blackwine wanted to reach the next valley before the midday sun blistered their skin. As they moved further south, the heat grew more intense and the sun burned like a huge furnace above their heads.

By mid-morning they could see the valley in the distance — it looked like another large crack in the red earth but, as with Grave Valley, there was a small canyon where they moored the ship out of the wind. A winding path led down into what Davin said was Narrow Valley. They zigzagged back and forth across a cliff face, each carrying a large bag that banged awkwardly on their backs. There would be no filling of water barrels here. The angled corners on the path wouldn't allow them to manoeuvre the long poles. Kiall prayed that whatever Blackwine was trading for this time would be small and light.

The villagers here were not as pleased to see them. They provided food and water, then disappeared, leaving just one man and one woman to manage the trading. Kiall felt uneasy, as if they were being watched. When he caught a glimpse of a man holding a spear hiding in the nearby forest, it confirmed his suspicions. These people had had dealings with Blackwine before and it didn't look as though they'd been amicable.

Strangely, Blackwine first arranged for them to sleep in the village overnight and then sent everyone off to amuse themselves while he bartered with the two villagers.

'What's he up to?' Kiall said to Maya. 'Let's hang around and watch.'

'We probably won't understand the language,' Maya said. 'How will we know what's going on?'

'I know someone we can ask.'

Kiall walked straight towards where he'd seen the villager with the spear, ready to retreat if the man attacked. But when he reached the first row of trees, no one was there. He and Maya hid in the undergrowth and watched Blackwine who seemed very angry, throwing his arms around and shouting. The two villagers didn't cower away — they merely stared at him in silence. When he'd calmed down a little, Blackwine brought out gold and silver, then the other bright trinkets he'd stolen, but the two shook their heads. Finally he reached for the bag that Portus had been carrying and took out two cutlasses and half a dozen daggers.

The two villagers examined them eagerly, testing the blade edges and conferring with each other. Then they shook hands with Blackwine and signalled someone behind them. Two more women came out of a large hut, carrying bulging sacks, which they dropped on the ground before scuttling back inside. Blackwine opened one of the sacks and cut off a piece of dark brown substance that he chewed for a few minutes. Nodding, he accepted a cup of water.

'That's got to be dried meat,' Maya said. 'Guess what we'll be eating for the next few weeks.'

'How tasty,' Kiall said sarcastically. 'Have you worked out yet how we're going to get back to the ship and cut up the sail?'

'We'll have to do it tonight while everyone's asleep. We need a knife though. Or something sharp.'

Kiall felt something poke him in the leg and turned to find the villager with the spear standing behind him. The man didn't look like the other villagers. He was dressed in a rough animal skin tunic and had two more skins tied around his feet. His hair was long and shaggy, as was his beard, but his spear was finely crafted with a lethal point on one end and carvings along its shaft.

Kiall and Maya scrambled to their feet. 'Good day,' Kiall said, at a loss as to what else he should say.

'Geerrgh,' the man said, and saluted them.

Maya saluted him back. 'Friends,' she said, patting her chest.

'I hope that's not a sign that you want to fight him,' Kiall said.

The man patted his own chest, then pointed to his mouth. 'Gorrr,' he said, then opened his mouth, showing them that instead of a tongue, he had a grisly stump. He pointed to the village, thumped his thigh and pointed into the forest, gesturing that they should follow him.

'I don't think we should,' Kiall said. 'He'll probably kill us and eat us.'

The man clearly understood what they were saying. He shook his head and patted his chest again. 'Hreerrrgh.'

'He wants to show us something,' Maya said.

'Yes, a large boiling pot.'

'No, I think it's safe.' Maya stepped forward and the man beamed, his teeth remarkably white and sound.

Kiall continued to grumble but he followed Maya and the man, wishing that he had one of the daggers that Blackwine had just traded away. The forest around them was full of noise and colour — bright-coloured birds swooped and dived, calling raucously, and insects buzzed and trilled. Bushes grew close to the track, their leaves large and floppy, their flowers all colours of the rainbow. The further the group walked, the hotter it became, but it was a damp heat that soaked their clothing, sweat trickling down their faces and backs.

At the edge of a clearing, they stopped and the man signalled them to stay hidden behind a large bush. He walked into the clearing and laid down his spear, then stood with his arms straight out from his sides. Suddenly two more men emerged from the wall of green on the other side, walked towards him and circled him twice before standing in front of him. All three gestured and grunted at each other.

'I don't think any of them have tongues,' Maya whispered. 'What happened? Who cut them out?'

'A punishment,' Kiall whispered back. 'But for what?'

A tiny woman now appeared and joined the men. Their guide pointed back at the twins and the woman beckoned them to approach. Kiall's heart pounded as they moved forward and joined the quartet.

'Who are you?' the tiny woman chirped.

'You can speak,' Maya said.

'Yes, I still have my tongue,' she said, smiling. 'Now please answer my question.'

'We're not pirates,' Maya said.

'We got captured by Blackwine and have been forced to work on his ship,' Kiall added.

Their guide made a long, garbled sound and

pretended to juggle between his two hands, then slashed one through the air.

'Blackwine is trading blades again.' The woman spat on the ground. 'I curse the day he found this valley.'

'Are you from the village?' Maya asked.

'Once we were,' the woman said. 'There were disputes over trading with Blackwine. We said we didn't need goods stolen from others, and it was his suggestion that any who didn't want to trade be banished from the village. Leaving more profit for the rest, of course.'

'What happened to their tongues?' Kiall said, and reddened, feeling maybe he'd been a little rude.

'Also Blackwine's suggestion.' The three men grunted and made low, sad noises. 'Our village chief thought it was a fitting punishment for those who spoke against him.'

'But you escaped the cutting?' Maya asked.

'I ran before they could catch me.' The woman held out her hand. 'I am Fortuna. This is Turn, Semill and Glash.'

After they'd shaken everyone's hands and introduced themselves, Kiall and Maya learned that the four outcasts were all that were left of more than twenty who had been mutilated and banished. They were planning to leave this part of the valley as soon as they could finish building a small boat that they had hidden further downriver from the village. Their destination was a large lake, many days journey away.

'You could climb the cliff and take Blackwine's ship,' Kiall said.

Fortuna shook her head. 'We have no wish to live up on the plain. It's a hard life, suited only to pirates and greedy traders.'

'But ...' Maya grinned. 'Do you have a sail for your little boat?'

'We have been trying to make one out of large plantain leaves,' Fortuna said. 'It takes a long time to sew them all together.'

'We know where you could get a large sail and cut it down to the size you need.' Maya glanced at Kiall. 'And we'll help you steal it, won't we?'

Kiall paled. 'We're going to *steal* the whole sail?'

'It's the perfect plan,' Maya said. 'We'll have enough sail cloth left to get back to the rift cave, but not enough for Blackwine to continue south. He really will be forced to go back to get another mainsail off a skyship.'

'It's not a perfect plan —' Kiall stepped back from Maya's punch. 'All right, it's perfect. But only if Fortuna and the others help.'

'You are serious?' Fortuna asked.

'Yes.'

'Then we will help. It means we can leave tomorrow.' The men around her grinned and patted each other on the back, then patted Kiall and Maya. Kiall thought he'd be bruised for days.

'We'd better go back to the village,' Maya said. 'Before anyone starts asking where we are.'

They bade farewell, arranging to meet at the foot of the cliff path when the moon was at its highest. Then Glash led them back along the track.

Near to the village, Kiall said, 'My shirt is soaked. I want a swim in the river.'

'That gives me an idea,' Maya said. 'We'll swim up to the village from further down and make it look like that's where we've been all this time.' They asked Glash to take them downriver and waved him goodbye, then stripped down to their undergarments and jumped into the cool water. The river was narrow and deep, with rapids at the next bend, and Kiall could feel the current tugging at his legs. He sat in the small, shallow cove and washed himself as best he could. Maya did the same, frowning each time she ventured out a little deeper.

'We won't be able to swim upstream. The river is too fast here.' She climbed the bank and pulled on her clothes, then finger-combed her wet hair and re-braided it tightly at the back of her head. At a rustling in the bushes, she spun around, fists up. Kiall got to his feet, feeling ridiculous in his wet under-trousers that clung to his legs.

Davin came out of the bushes, a large grin on his face. 'I wondered where you two were. Blackwine wouldn't like it if he thought you'd run away.'

'How would he catch us?' Kiall said.

'The villagers are expert trackers when you pay them enough gold.' Davin shrugged. 'But here you are. You weren't thinking of swimming, were you?'

'No,' Maya said. 'We can't swim.' It was a lie, probably unnecessary, but she felt compelled to say it anyway. The weaker and more helpless they looked, the less likely that anyone would expect them to escape.

'Doesn't everyone in Quentaris swim?' Davin said.

'No. What for?' Kiall said.

'I don't know, I just thought ... that people in Quentaris could do anything. Swim, dance, sing, be free.' He blushed and turned away. 'Stupid of me.'

Maya touched his arm. 'No, it's not.'

But Davin snatched his arm away and strode off, crashing through the bushes, leaving Maya and Kiall to grimace at each other. When they were both dressed again, they made their way back to the village. Although it wasn't very late in the afternoon, half of the valley was already in deep shadow and the villagers appeared to be eating their evening meal. They made room for the twins around the central cooking fire. Several nodded greetings, but no one spoke to them. They could see Blackwine in one of the huts, being waited on with plates of roasted meat and vegetables, and the pirates in another hut sharing a whole haunch between them.

Kiall and Maya drank the offered water from carved wooden goblets, but after the meal was finished one of the women passed around a large tray of small, burnished metal cups. Another woman followed her, carrying a leather bottle from which she poured a clear liquid. The villagers greeted the filling of their cups with great delight, raising their arms high and cheering, then downing the drink in one swallow. Kiall sniffed his and said to Maya, 'It's some kind of spirit. Smells like lamp oil. I don't want to drink it but ...'

'We don't want to offend anyone,' she finished.

The villagers didn't mind at all that the twins weren't drinking. Their cups were taken from them by their neighbours and the contents swallowed at once. The bottle came around again and again, and soon everyone was swaying and singing, and some staggered off to their huts. Blackwine and the pirates had their own bottles; the liquor was obviously very strong as they also shortly keeled over and began snoring.

'This is too good to be true,' Kiall said. 'Everyone so drunk that they'll never notice us sneaking off to the ship.'

'Not so fast,' Maya said. 'Look over there, on that hillock by the river, and at the edge of the forest.'

Kiall squinted through the gloomy dusk and saw what she meant. The villagers had set sentries — probably in case the banished ones came to steal food — and they had not been drinking. 'Curses! How will we get past the one at the river? He's right where the cliff path begins.'

'A diversion,' Maya said. 'Let's stroll down to the water and wash our hands and faces.' On the way, she murmured, 'Look around as though you're curious about the valley. See if there are any other sentries.'

At the river's edge, Kiall squatted and rinsed his hands and face in the cold water. 'Only those two, I think.'

'Check again on the way back.'

As they walked back, she pointed at the trees and said loudly, 'They must be good lumber trees. Very straight and tall.'

'They'd make fine ship's masts too,' Kiall said, trying to scan the south end of the village as well.

'They do.' Davin stepped from Blackwine's hut, giving them both a fright.

'Have you been in there all this time?' Maya asked.

'Yes. Why?' Davin said.

'I didn't see you, that's all. Did you eat?'

'Of course.' He eyed them curiously. 'You aren't drunk.'

'Neither are you,' Maya said.

'We won't have sore heads tomorrow, then, will we?' Davin said. 'You'd better get some sleep. Tomorrow will be hard work, especially if everyone else is in an abominable mood.'

'Where are our beds?' Kiall asked.

'Look in any hut. The villagers here put out mats and you sleep wherever you find a space.'

'What about you?'

'I get to sleep in the captain's hut.' He smiled wryly. 'Lucky me. I have to guard his sword and dagger. The villagers would be quite happy to get some for nothing.'

'Well, goodnight then,' Maya said. She turned and walked towards the huts furthest away from Blackwine's.

Kiall followed, feeling Davin's eyes on his back. The boy was sharp, and not to be taken for a fool. And, Kiall realised, he was hiding something.

They reached a hut and Maya checked inside. 'We need to sleep by the door,' she said softly.

'Davin's up to something,' Kiall said.

'What makes you think that? Has he said something?'

'No, it's more what he doesn't say.' Kiall scratched his neck. 'He acts like he's a servant of some kind, or an apprentice pirate, if there is such a thing. But there's something strange about him, and it sets my teeth on edge.'

'Is this your famous instinct again?' Maya said, grinning.

Kiall huffed. 'There's nothing wrong with my instinct. That's how I saved you when that horse bolted in the street.'

'True.' Maya sobered. 'You're right. There is something peculiar about him, but I doubt he'll confess if we ask. We'll have to watch and wait — and we won't trust him either.' She mimed turning a key between her lips. 'Not a word in his presence.'

'Exactly.'

'Let's try the next hut. This one is full.'

There were spaces near the door at the next hut and they sank down onto the thick rush mats, which were surprisingly comfortable. 'I'm so tired,' Maya whispered. 'We'll have to prod each other awake.'

'Have you worked out how to get past the river sentry yet?'

'Setting a hut on fire won't work. It'll wake everyone up.'

'How about a small fire to the north of him? He'll have to go and investigate it, won't he?'

'Good plan, brother!' Maya said.

'See, I can make plans, too.'

'If one of us can't get past the sentry, the other must go ahead anyway. Fortuna and her friends will be able to carry the sail.'

Having decided on their tactics, Kiall and Maya lay back to wait. It was Kiall's idea to play some of the old guessing games they hadn't competed in since they were little, and it kept them awake until they judged it was time to make a move.

Maya agreed to light the diversion fire — if she couldn't get back to the meeting place, Kiall would climb the cliff path and help the others steal the sail. She searched the hut for something in which to carry the cooking fire embers, but all she could find was a pile of the small metal cups. In the end, she decided to put a coal in each one and wrap them in her shirt, carrying them carefully so they wouldn't burn holes in the cloth.

Kiall waited by the hut, trying to stay calm, but it was as if an icy hand rested on his neck. What if Blackwine caught them? He kept seeing the cutlass swinging, the severed head bouncing on the ground. Maybe they could just wait it out. Maybe Blackwine would return to the rift cave and let them go …

Why was Maya taking so long to start the fire? He strained to see any sign of flames. Surely the sentry would smell the smoke? But the sentry seemed to have gone to sleep, his head drooping to his chest, and no matter how Kiall willed him to stand and look around, he didn't move.

'Kiall!' Maya was right behind him. 'He's asleep. We can creep past him if we're quiet.'

'After all that —' Kiall's legs felt wobbly and he took a deep breath. 'Never mind. Let's go.'

They crept around the back of the huts and across to the river bank where the path began, only ten feet away from the sentry. As they passed him, they heard a buzzing noise — he was snoring — and knew if he stopped, they were in trouble. However, they were soon out of earshot, so they broke into a fast trot. Kiall hoped that Fortuna was waiting as promised, with a knife, otherwise he wasn't sure how they'd cut up the sail on their own.

At the bottom of the cliff, four shadows hovered. 'We thought your courage had failed,' Fortuna said.

Kiall decided to save his breath and didn't answer. He set off up the cliff path, one hand touching the rock face so he didn't stray too close to the edge. His lungs were on fire before they were halfway up, but he would rest at the top. There was no time to waste. If they were discovered missing from the village, and the sail was gone, punishment would be instantaneous and fatal.

It felt like hours before they reached the top of the cliff. He staggered away from the path and fell to the ground, his heart thumping wildly in his ears.

'Come on, where is the ship?' Fortuna pulled him up and pushed him forward. Kiall blinked and searched the darkness ahead but could see nothing. Had Blackwine slipped away in the night and left them behind?

'Kiall — over there!' Maya tugged his arm and pointed off to the left. He made out a spike above the rocks. It was the mast, thanks to the gods. They ran across to the *Shiba* and Glash climbed on board first to check there was no sentry. As Kiall waited by the ladder, his skin began to prickle and he sniffed the air, dread stealing over him. 'It's the cat,' he said. 'Everyone — get on the ship — now!'

Maya scrambled to the ladder and raced upwards, swinging her leg over the rail and then leaning down to haul the others up faster. Kiall waited to go last, the stench growing stronger by the second, and then he heard the low howl not more than twenty feet away. That was why there was no sentry. He leapt up the ladder, bumping Turn's heels, knowing that any moment the cat would be clawing at his legs or sinking its teeth into him. A bite from that animal would mean an agonising death from putrefaction, that's if he kept it away from his neck.

'Eeerrgggggh.' Turn stopped, his foot caught in the rope loops, and the whole ladder shuddered as he struggled to free himself. The howl spiralled upwards, a death cry. Panic burned through Kiall's mind, and he clutched at the ladder, unable to go up or down.

7
Double Trickery

'HERE.' MAYA LEANT DOWN from the rail, past the scrambling Turn, and handed Kiall a pike. He gripped it in his right hand, turned and stabbed blindly downwards, over and over, not caring if he struck the cat or not, wanting only to get it away from him.

Something sharp went through his left boot and he wondered if he'd stabbed himself, then the pike connected with a solid *thunk* and the howl changed to a scream. The stench seared Kiall's throat and he gagged while still thrusting the pike below him, unsure what had happened. Then there was nothing — no smell, no sounds, no movement on the ground.

He waited, pike at the ready, for several long seconds. The ladder above him was finally clear and Maya called, 'Climb up. Quickly.'

He needed no second command. In moments he was sprawled on the deck, gasping, the pike beside him. Maya examined it, sniffing then touching the sharp end. 'Blood. It smells disgusting. You must have got the beast.'

Kiall groaned and sat up. 'How are we going to explain that to Blackwine?'

'We're not,' Maya said. 'We were never here, remember? We're asleep in our hut right now.'

Above them, Fortuna and Glash worked on the yardarm, slashing ties while the other two waited on the deck to catch the sail and fold it up. Kiall and Maya raided the stores for food to give to Fortuna and her men, packing it into sacks. When all were ready to leave the ship, Kiall hesitated.

'Glash will go first,' Fortuna said. 'He has good

night eyes and will see the cat before you do. Give him the pike.'

Kiall gladly handed it over and they waited, holding their breath. Glash climbed carefully down to the ground, watching for the cat, ready to defend himself. But nothing happened, and the others followed, all staying alert just in case.

'Do you think I killed it?' Kiall asked Maya.

'I hope so,' she said.

'It doesn't matter,' Fortuna said. 'All of this can be blamed on us. You need only say you saw one of us in the forest yesterday, watching you. They will be angry that you didn't tell them, that is all.'

'What if they track you and catch you?'

She shrugged. 'We're leaving tonight. We have supplies now, and can make our sail later. The first part of the river is fast so we won't need it yet. Don't worry — the villagers will only pursue us a short way. They don't care enough about Blackwine to do his bidding any further.'

'Not even for gold?'

'For his gold, they will pretend a great search and find nothing but our leavings. They will be glad to see us gone.'

'Oooorrrggg,' Glash said.

'Yes, we must hurry,' Fortuna said. She slung a sack over her shoulder and headed for the cliff path. Glash took two more sacks and the other two men shared the sail between them. Kiall and Maya brought up the rear with nothing to carry. The trip back to the valley bottom was silent, each concentrating on staying on the path and not over-balancing. At the base of the cliff, the twins embraced the four and watched them slide off into the darkness. Within seconds they were gone.

'Now we have to sneak back without being caught,' Maya whispered. 'I hope that guard is still asleep.'

'Follow me,' Kiall said. Only now that the worst of the risks were over did he feel a burning in his left foot as he crept along the path to the river. The huts came into view. If only he could go down to the water, take his boot off and bathe his foot, but how would he explain it? He would have to wait until morning.

Soon he was limping badly, and Maya caught his arm. 'What's the matter?' she whispered.

'Ssh. Nothing. Let's just get to the hut.' Kiall kept walking, staying low, watching for the spot where the guard had been when they left. But he wasn't there. They stopped and waited, scanning the river bank and around the huts.

Maya nudged him. 'There.' The guard was coming back from behind the first hut, pulling at his trousers. He must have left his post to relieve himself. He sat down on the hillock again, gazed around for a few seconds, then lowered his head to his chest. A few minutes later, his snoring drifted across the open ground again.

'In Quentaris, he'd be put in the dungeons for that,' Kiall said.

'Just be grateful,' Maya said.

They stayed low and tiptoed around the bushes to the end hut, then made their way from one to the next until they reached their sleeping hut. Collapsing on the mats, Kiall wriggled his toes inside his left boot and pain shot through his foot. It felt sodden, and his heart sank. He wondered how much blood was still seeping out. The cat must have got a claw or a tooth into him.

'Maya,' he said, poking her.

'Hmmm?' She was nearly asleep. How could she?

'I have to soak my foot. It's getting painful.'

'You can't.'

'My boot will be bloody. How will I explain that

in the morning? I have to wash it, too.'

Silence while she thought. 'All right, but be careful. Pretend you're hot or thirsty or something.'

He crawled out of the hut and crept down to the river. If the guard woke and saw him, that would be a problem but it was worth the risk.

With his boot off, the burning subsided a little, but he had to bite his lip when dipping his foot into the cold water. The pain changed to a fiery throbbing that eventually eased a little. He could then rinse out his boot, deciding to wet both so it wouldn't look suspicious. He could say he fell in, perhaps.

Peering down at his foot, he examined the wound and tried to work out how serious it might be. The gash was small but deep, as if from a thin dagger. Was it poisoned? Too early to say, but the animal's stench was ominous. On the other hand, he hoped he'd killed the thing and that cheered him up. And the mainsail was gone. Blackwine must surely return to the cave now. Morning would likely answer all questions.

Back in the hut, Maya was fast asleep. Kiall tried to join her but between the churning worry in his mind and the pain in his foot, he lay, eyes wide open, until dawn. The villagers stirred slowly and rose to build up the cooking fire for the first meal. A large pot of bubbling brown grain looked unappetising but the twins were glad of the bowls of hot food they were given, finding it both filled them and warmed them up, readying them for whatever came next.

Blackwine emerged from his hut while they were still eating and ordered the pirates to get everything ready for departure. He ignored the twins but, after he'd said his farewell to the relieved-looking villagers, he snapped, 'Join the line', at them. Davin stood, glaring, until Kiall and Maya were filing meekly along the track.

'How's your foot?' Maya murmured.

'Bearable,' Kiall said. 'I wish my boots were dry.'

'Why? What did you do to them?' Davin asked.

Curses! Kiall thought. The boy is always eavesdropping or spying on us.

'Fell into the water,' he said aloud. 'Missed my footing when I went to fill my bottle.'

'Where is your bottle?' Davin said.

'Here, on my belt.' The bottle was empty and Kiall hoped Davin wouldn't demand to check it.

'Your boots will dry in the sun,' Davin said. 'You can take them off on the ship.'

'They're probably nearly dry already,' Maya said. In front of Kiall, her shoulders were rigid with tension. Kiall knew how she felt. His own heart was leaping about under his ribs like a crazy caged pigeon.

They climbed the cliff path, straggling at the rear, not wanting to be too close when Blackwine discovered the missing sail. As it was, he didn't notice. Instead, when they arrived at the ship, the captain and the pirates were searching around the rocks and out on the plain, Blackwine whistling over and over for his cat.

'Have you seen it?' Davin asked them.

'No. Maybe it ran off,' Kiall said.

'It guards the ship. It always has.' Davin peered at the bottom of the ladder. 'There's blood here. And there.' He pointed at the ground. 'Something attacked it.'

'More likely it attacked someone,' Maya said.

'You think we've had thieves?' Davin said. His mouth pinched tight and he leapt up the ladder like a monkey. They could hear him thumping down the steps and into the hold, then there was a long silence followed by more footsteps. A few minutes later, he appeared on the deck above them. 'There's food missing,' he said, 'but our cargo is safe. Cursed villagers!'

'That's all right then,' Kiall said.

'It won't be if our captain can't find his cat.'

Suddenly, a roar of rage echoed from the plain and Davin's head shot up. His hand trembled as he wiped his face and stared out across the red earth. As Blackwine and the pirates came into view, he shuddered. 'Oh, gods, no. I can't …'

'What? What's wrong?' Kiall asked, knowing full well what Blackwine had found.

Davin was silent, his eyes focused on the approaching group. Kiall turned to see Blackwine carrying a limp, furry body, his face twisted with fury. When he reached the ship, he screamed at Davin to throw down a blanket, and then laid the cat gently onto the patterned cloth, stroking its head and crooning to it. The cat's fur had lost much of its colour, turning a dirty beige, and two bloody, dust-caked holes could be seen in its neck and shoulder. After a few minutes, Blackwine folded the blanket over and around the cat, then stood, glaring around at the crew.

'If I find out that any of you had a part in this, I will tear you to shreds with my bare hands.' His eyes fixed on Kiall as if he knew who the culprit was, but Kiall stood unflinching. There was no way Blackwine could know he was responsible, and he'd lie a thousand times to avoid being found out.

Davin spoke up. 'There's food missing. Those villagers are the guilty ones. I told you not to trust them.'

'Don't be a fool!' Blackwine spat. 'Why would the villagers steal our stores? They have far better food in the valley.'

'What about the banished ones?'

'They are all dead.'

'Now who is being foolish?' Davin said. 'I saw one of them in the forest. The villagers just told you that to make themselves appear in charge.'

Kiall wondered if he should say he'd also seen one of the banished people. Blackwine turned on him in an instant. 'You — I can tell you know something. Did you see this man?'

'Er … I think so. I saw someone hiding …'

'Why didn't you tell anyone?' Blackwine's face was dark red with rage. 'If those scum have stolen our gold or cloth —'

'It's all safe,' Davin said quickly. 'It's just the food.'

Just when Kiall thought no one would ever notice the sail, Portus looked up. 'Ho, where's our mainsail gone?'

'What?' Blackwine screeched, peering upwards. 'Those festering bloodsuckers! How dare they? We're going back to the village. We're going to kill the whole lot of them. We're going to burn every hut and put a stake through every child. We're —'

'What for? The villagers didn't do this. You said so yourself.' Davin was pale with fear but he wasn't about to back off.

'We'll track down the banished ones then. Spit and gut them like goats!' Blackwine paced up and down beside the ship. 'Cut off their heads and make bowls out of them for pigs to eat from.'

Maya coughed. 'I saw some strange people yesterday. When we were downriver, washing our clothes and getting water.'

'And?' Blackwine leaned towards her, his face inches away as he glowered at her.

'They had a boat. They were p-packing it. Ready to leave.' She swallowed hard. 'They are likely well gone by now. Down that fast river.'

'Pah!' Blackwine spat a great gob on her boot. 'Useless.'

'If she's right, there is no point in us going back down there again,' Davin said. 'The villagers will be glad to be rid of the banished ones. They won't help us.'

'They'll help if I tell them to!' Blackwine said.

'We'll just waste time, and who knows what else will be stolen while we are chasing phantoms? We have to keep sailing.'

Blackwine seemed to calm down unnaturally fast. He stared at his cat in its covering. 'We must bury Sly. That is what we must do.'

Kiall thought the man was a lunatic — why couldn't he just leave the cat and go back for another sail? But that would be too easy, and nothing in this hot, terrible world was easy. The whole crew was made to help dig a grave for the cat in the hard, rocky soil, using pikes and axes to make a shallow hole. Blackwine placed the cat into the grave and covered it with earth, then lay on top and cried softly. Kiall almost felt guilty except that the pain in his foot was getting worse, and when Blackwine saw the wound, he would know exactly what caused it. Then Kiall's head would leave his shoulders, and that would probably be the end of Maya, too.

He gritted his teeth and tried not to limp on his way back to the *Shiba*. They were all sweaty and dusty from the digging, and there was no water to spare for washing. He shook the dust out of his shirt and put it on again, then found some shade to sit in while they waited for Blackwine to come back from his mourning.

Maya sat beside him and whispered, 'When they talk about the sail, we'd better stay quiet. Davin is suspicious, and Blackwine is mad.'

Kiall nodded. Maya made sense, as usual.

The sun was nearly at its highest point when Blackwine finally climbed back on board and inspected the space where the mainsail used to be.

'We can still sail without it,' he said to Davin and Portus. 'But we'll be slow.'

'How will we manage in the Southern Squalls?' Davin asked. 'We'll turn over without that sail.'

'I said I would be at Silven Canyon before Callan's Moon rises,' Blackwine said. 'It's worth too much to risk not getting there in time. Silven and his village have promised me ten egg sapphires.'

'I've looked at the maps,' Davin said. 'We always go the same way, with the same trading stops. If we go back to the skyship and get a new sail, we can head directly south, past Yellow Rocks. We can still make it in time, and then we could go on to the mines.'

'What would you know?' Blackwine snapped. 'Idiot!'

Davin's face flamed but his mouth tightened. 'Without a mainsail, we cannot attack a single ship. We would have no manoeuvring ability, and not enough speed to catch anyone.'

Piracy was obviously still Blackwine's first love — his eyes gleamed and he nodded. 'Maybe the idiot speaks sense, hey?' He smiled at Davin but it was not a comrade's smile, nor even a praising one. It looked to Kiall more like the smile one forces before stabbing a friend. He shivered.

As before, the crew had to haul the ship out of its mooring place and onto the plain in order to catch the wind. The journey north was not going to be easy; Kiall had his question about the wind answered and there was a lot of arduous tacking back and forth across the red expanse to try and catch the gusts. Strings of curses and oaths erupted each time a wind died and they were forced to wait. Kiall, Maya and the rest of the pirates were run ragged as they battled to follow shouted orders that had them swapping between ropes and tightening or loosening lines.

But beyond his exhaustion and the agony of his foot, jubilation grew as they edged closer and closer to the rift cave. The gods only knew how they would get away from Blackwine when they got there; there was no point worrying about that yet. Just before dusk of the following day, they caught a late squall that thrust them forward and landed them at the mountain base as darkness fell.

Everyone looked worn to a thread, and Blackwine's temper had grown worse in the past two days, if that were possible. His shouts often escalated to shrieks, and there were several long scratches on his chest where he'd torn at his cat tattoo as he grieved for the animal's loss. Even if they hadn't been so desperate to get back to Quentaris, Kiall would have wanted to escape from the *Shiba* before Blackwine went totally insane and killed them all.

'Eat!' Blackwine shouted, after they had moored. 'We sail again at dawn. Davin, you and Portus get the new sail from Finny's ship. If Finny argues, run him through.'

Davin looked taken aback at this command.

Finny captained the skyship, and he stood on his upper deck, watching the *Shiba* curiously. He was a huge, shambling creature with a lantern jaw and two lethal scimitars at his belt, and next to him Davin would be easily dwarfed.

Blackwine went down to the hold and came back with two bottles of spirits, then disappeared into his cabin and slammed the door.

Davin made a rude sign at the door. 'That's right, you drink and leave the work to me. You two!' He gestured to Kiall and Maya. 'Come and help me with the sail while Portus fixes the rigging.'

Kiall followed Davin and Maya to the skyship, gazing up at the huge rotors fore and aft. They looked like giant fans, and he realised that the wind they made would propel the skyship no matter what the weather. Finny met them in the hold, his arms folded, pale, worm-like skin stretched tightly over his jaw.

'What 'ee want now?' he grumbled.

'Blackwine needs a sail,' Davin said.

'I need my sails,' Finny said, shaking his head. 'Out tonight, us are. No moon in Quentaris.'

'Blackwine needs a sail,' Davin repeated. 'He won't take no for an answer.'

'Won't he now?' Finny grinned, his teeth clacking. He rested a hand on one of his scimitars and glanced at Maya. 'She for swap?'

'No,' Davin said. 'You'd better give over the sail. Blackwine is ... his cat is dead. He's ... on edge.'

Finny flinched, and a slimy sheen of sweat appeared on his skin. 'Cat dead? He ... slash 'ee?'

'Not me. But anyone who defies him now ...'

'Spare sail in back hold. 'Ee wait.' Finny whistled shrilly and two sky pirates climbed down a ladder from the upper deck. The hair on Kiall's neck prickled at the sight of the monstrous bony things, with eye sockets like bottomless pits. No wonder children in Quentaris had nightmares if they happened to see one on a dark night. The pirates hauled the sail across the deck and dumped it in front of Davin, who nodded his thanks and signalled Kiall and Maya to help him carry it over to the *Shiba*. It took the three of them and Portus another two hours to get the sail up and properly rigged and tied. Only then were the twins allowed to go and find something to eat. They foraged in the galley and found food, then sat in the bow.

Kiall propped up his throbbing foot on the edge of a hatch, too scared to take his boot off and look at it. He concentrated on eating. 'Yuck. Dried meat and water,' he said, chewing something that was more like leather than meat.

'Take extra and put it in your pocket,' Maya said. 'It might be a long night.'

'How are we going to get away?'

'Or more correctly, how are we going to get away and take some treasure with us?' Maya said, with a sparkle in her eyes.

'Are you crazy?' Kiall said. 'What happened to planning and caution? We just want to get home.'

'What? Come all this way for nothing? Not likely,' Maya said. 'The risk is worth it. Certain people in Quentaris are going to pay for what they've done to our family.'

Kiall stared at her determined face and felt the old boldness and resolve surge up inside him. 'Yes, they are. The Tigran family of Quentaris will rise again.'

'Only if you help me first,' Davin said behind them.

8
Battle
for Gold

KIALL AND MAYA SWUNG around to find Davin right behind them. 'You're a filthy spy,' Kiall said. 'I suppose you're going to tell Blackwine now.'

'Not if you do what I want,' Davin said.

'You want us to kill Blackwine and make you captain?' Kiall said sarcastically.

'I want you to take me with you to Quentaris and vouchsafe me — help me set up a trading business.'

Davin stood, arms folded, waiting for their reply.

'I thought you were a pirate,' Maya said. 'This is your life, you said.'

'No, I said it's *a* life. But not for me. Do you really think I'd want to spend the rest of my years roaming this blasted world, killing and stealing?'

'Well, yes,' Kiall said. 'You seem to do well at it.'

Davin snorted. 'Out of necessity. Now I want something better.'

'We don't know how *we're* going to get back to Quentaris yet, let alone whether we can take you with us,' Maya said.

'I have a plan,' Davin said.

'Hmmm, is that so?' Kiall said, nudging Maya.

'Let him speak,' Maya said. 'But speak softly. There are always ears where you least expect them.'

Davin leant forward. 'In the caves, Blackwine has a locked storeroom where he keeps his treasure. He keeps it separate from the others.' Kiall raised his eyebrows in disbelief but Davin ignored him and continued. 'I have a key to the room. I propose we take what is most valuable and easy to carry, and board Finny's skyship. But we will have to hurry. He is getting ready to leave.'

'You'll share the treasure with us?' Kiall said.

'Why should we trust you?'

'I want to go to Quentaris more than you will ever understand.'

'Explain, then.'

Davin's mouth tightened into a hard line. 'I cannot. But if you do not help me, I will steal the treasure and go anyway, and take my chances that no one in Quentaris will think I'm a villain or a pirate. And besides, do you want me to tell Blackwine about the wound in your foot? I'm sure he'd like to know how you got it.'

'You piece of mule dung,' Kiall said.

'Your insults are wasting time,' Davin said. 'We either go to the storeroom now, or it will be too late. Do you want to be forced back onto the plains tomorrow?'

'No,' Kiall said. 'All right, we agree. But if you doublecross us, you will pay, one way or another. A Tigran never forgets those who cause us harm.'

'Let's go then.' Davin made for the rail and was down the ladder in seconds, waiting impatiently for the twins to catch up. As soon as they joined him, he headed up a rocky path towards the cave entrance. Kiall's limp was getting worse, and his foot felt the size of a giant's, jammed inside his boot.

At this rate, he'd have to cut the leather to get it off.

Just inside the cave entrance, a sky pirate sat on a rock, picking his teeth with a small narrow blade and wiping it on his shirt. His sunken eyes rotated slightly to scrutinise the three of them and a scaly tongue licked the edge of his gaping mouth.

'Where 'ee go?' his voice grated.

'Blackwine wants more cutlasses from his store.' Davin stared the sky pirate down. 'We'll not touch your booty. Let us past.'

The pirate shrugged and his bones clacked. Davin led the way past him, head in the air, but Kiall could feel the pirate's beady eyes watching them all the way down the path. Once they'd turned the corner, a wave of relief washed over him. Davin kept walking, turning left and right down corridors hewn out of the rock until Kiall thought he'd never find the way out on his own.

They passed caves filled with tumbled piles of gold and silver plates, cups and candlesticks, and chests of plundered goods, but Davin stopped at a wooden door. He rammed a key into the lock, turned it and pushed the door open. They stepped into a huge, dark room that appeared empty at first; Davin lit a taper and went to a large lamp on a table in the middle of the floor. As the lamp began to glow, the room gradually became visible and the twins gasped.

When it came to treasure, it seemed Blackwine was a very orderly person. Gold plates, goblets, platters and bowls were neatly stacked along one wall. Two large chests held gold and silver pieces, jewelled ornaments and bolts of glittering cloth lay in tidy rows on shelves, and more shelves held dozens of small, bulging bags. Empty bags, sacks and chests were piled near the door, ready to hold more treasure. Kiall couldn't believe his eyes. He was sure even the Archon of Quentaris or the highest nobles didn't have this much wealth in their storerooms.

Davin was clearly familiar with what was in the room. He went swiftly to the shelves of bags and selected four, then picked a sack off the pile and threw handfuls of gold pieces into it. 'Hurry up, you two,' he snapped. 'Take a sack and help yourselves. Those small bags are full of jewels, mostly uncut. The cut ones are in the smallest bags.'

Kiall didn't hesitate. He grabbed a sack and half-filled it with gold while Maya selected half a dozen jewel bags. The gold was heavy and he wondered if he should put some back, but greed took over and he kept it all.

'Are you ready?' Davin said. 'Come on, we must get back to the skyship.'

'Going somewhere?' a voice drawled from the doorway.

Kiall spun around, fear stabbing through him. Blackwine stood just inside the room, his sword hanging loosely from his hand, the cat tattoo gleaming in the lamplight. From the glitter in the captain's eyes, Kiall guessed that they would not leave the storeroom alive. What was a little more blood over this plunder that had plenty spilled over it already?

Davin gave a strangled cry. 'Let us go! We will leave your cursed gold behind, if that's what you want. Just let me go.' The last words were an anguished plea.

'Just let *you* go. That's not very nice for your new friends to hear. It suits you for them to die instead, does it?' Blackwine smiled but there was no amusement in it.

'That's not what I meant,' Davin said.

'I think it likely was,' Blackwine said. 'After all, I'd lay odds that you haven't told them about who you really are.'

Kiall stared at Davin, puzzled. 'Who are you then?'

'This fine lad is my son.' Blackwine grinned widely at the twins' reaction. 'Can't see the family likeness?' He stopped smiling. 'No, neither can I. If I had to spawn something, I hoped it would be something more like a man than a mule.'

'I have served you well,' Davin said through clenched teeth.

'You have indeed. You've given me an excellent reason to cut off three heads, all in one day, and you know how I enjoy that.' He whipped his cutlass through the air. 'I would enjoy it even more if my beloved Sly was here to suck out your eyeballs and chew your ears. She would think this an apt revenge, for my heart tells me it was one of you that killed her.'

Davin had dropped his sack and edged backwards. 'Just get it over with, will you? I'm sick to death of listening to your ravings.'

'Then you shall be first, my traitorous child.' Blackwine lifted his cutlass and moved forward on light feet, the cat tattoo rippling as if it were alive.

Davin took another step back and seized a sword off a shelf behind him. Its blade was short and broad. Its jewelled hilt glittered as he swung it up into defence. Kiall and Maya scuttled back out of the way as the two blades slashed, met and rang like bells. They were gradually nearing the door and Kiall realised they could slip out unheeded, leaving the monster and his son to fight it out.

'We can lock them in and make a run for it,' Kiall whispered to Maya.

'We can't leave Davin to die,' Maya said.

Why not? Kiall battled with himself for a few moments, but Maya was right. Shame burned inside him as he watched Davin fiercely parrying with all his strength. 'How can we help? There are no more swords, even if you or I were skilled enough, which we're not.'

The fight came dangerously close and they ducked behind Davin, then moved to the other side of the room, right by the door. Kiall glanced around for a weapon, anything at all, but there was nothing. He picked up a candelabrum and threw it at Blackwine but he dodged it easily. Maya hurled two plates and Blackwine swung his cutlass at her head, barely missing. She staggered backwards. Davin's eyes were fixed on Blackwine but the captain seemed to have no trouble fending off the twins while he fought. The two blades clanged and sparked, and the swordsmen were breathing hard, hoarse gasps accompanying each thrust.

Blackwine suddenly slashed left and right, catching Davin on the upper arm. Blood soaked his sleeve in a rush and his face paled, but he spat out, 'Don't think you have me beaten yet, you dog.'

'But I will beat you,' Blackwine said. 'And I will rid myself of a son I never wanted or needed.'

'You think I want or need you? You are the lowest of mongrels. I'm ashamed to come from you. My mother must have been insane.' Davin cut down and across, slicing Blackwine's thigh. Now both fighters leaked blood.

'Insane to keep you instead of killing you at birth,' Blackwine said.

They battled furiously again, back and forth across the room, seeing only each other and the hate that flashed in their eyes.

Kiall sensed the fight was slowly going against Davin. If Blackwine won, that would be the end of all of them. Kiall's foot caught in something sticking out from under the pile of sacks and he knelt, pulling at it.

'I'm going to try and get around behind Davin,'

Maya said. 'There's a heavy candlestick on that shelf.'

Kiall pulled desperately at the mesh around his boot and finally freed it. 'Don't be stupid. He'd cut you down in a second. What's this?' From under the sacks, he tugged out a thick net, as large as a bed-cover.

'I've seen the guards use these,' Maya said excitedly. 'In their battle practice. If you throw it over someone and hold it down, they can't move.'

'It won't be enough,' Kiall said. 'Blackwine might cut his way out. We'll need this, too.' He grabbed the largest sack and laid it ready, then glanced back at the two fighting. 'Oh gods, we're too late!'

Blackwine had broken through Davin's defence. The boy was down on one knee, his left hand over a wide cut across his chest. Blood dripped through his fingers and he wheezed as he tried to catch his breath. Blackwine stood over him gloating. 'Now you'll die like the mongrel you are,' he snarled.

'Take that corner,' Kiall commanded. 'Now!'

Together they lifted the net at the two front corners and ran across the room, just as Blackwine began to slice down. The net rose up in the air and came down over Blackwine's head, trapping his arms and tangling the cutlass.

'Pull back,' Kiall shouted, 'and around.' Together, they pulled the net down and took up the other corner, running towards each other, Maya just managing to duck under Kiall's arms. She took the corner Kiall thrust at her and tried to hold the bottom of the net tight, but Blackwine had twisted around and was flailing his arms wildly, pulling the net from her grip. He tried to raise his cutlass.

'Hold on!' Kiall shouted. He ran up behind Blackwine with the open sack and propelled it over his head, dragging it downwards as hard as he could, forcing it over the pirate's shoulders and down to his hips. Blackwine staggered, sight gone, and overbalanced, falling heavily on the floor. He shouted incoherently, struggling to free himself, thrashing about like a madman.

'We have to get out of here,' Kiall said.

'Not without Davin,' Maya said. 'Or some treasure. We can manage both if we hurry.'

Without another word, Kiall pulled Davin to his feet, but the boy was incapable of walking on his own. He sagged and Kiall had to put both arms around him and drag him to the door. He felt blood soak the front of his shirt but it hardly mattered right now. Maya had grabbed her sack and towed it behind her to the door and out into the corridor. When Kiall and Davin were out too, she pulled the door shut and turned the key.

'Thank the gods Davin left it in the door,' she said, puffing.

They could still hear Blackwine shouting, but it was distant and muffled now. No one would hear him until they came near the door. Kiall glanced around. 'Do you know the way out? I don't think Davin will be able to show us.'

'I think so. I counted as we came in, just in case.'

Kiall stared at her in admiration. 'You are amazing.'

'Just remember that when we get back to Quentaris and you're calling me an idiot as usual.' Her smile faded as she looked at Davin. 'He's in a bad way. The bleeding has slowed but ...'

Davin's eyelids flickered. 'I'll be fine ...' he whispered. 'Get me to the skyship.'

'Your wish is our command,' Kiall said.

The trip back to the cave entrance seemed to take forever, Kiall struggling between half-carrying Davin and limping heavily with pain shooting through his foot. Kiall grew convinced that the skyship would have left without them, but when they reached the last corner and he peered around it, the sky pirate was still on guard.

'Now what do we do?' Kiall said to the others.

'Put me down,' Davin muttered. When Kiall had lowered him to the ground, he said, 'When Finny gives the signal to leave, the guard will go to the ship to help put up the sails. Then we have about three minutes to get on board before they come back down and shut the hold door.' He coughed. 'That's if they follow the usual routine. If they don't ...'

No one wanted to think about that. Davin's chest wound was bleeding profusely. While they waited, Kiall took off his shirt and ripped it apart, fashioning it into a long scarf that he wrapped around Davin as tightly as he could. At least the cut in his arm was not too bad.

A sharp whistle startled them and Davin whispered, 'Finny. Ready?'

Kiall checked the guard and, sure enough, he was leaving, heading for the skyship. 'Time for us to go too,' Kiall said, helping Davin up. While they'd been waiting, he'd wondered where they were going to hide in the hold. Coming from

Quentaris, there had been boxes and chests and furs to use for concealment. Going back, the hold would be empty. Even if they got onto the ship, they'd be found as soon as a pirate came down the ladder.

There was no point thinking about it yet. Wait until they got on board — one problem at a time.

Outside the cave, darkness had fallen completely and the path was a faint blur. Kiall and Maya linked arms behind Davin's back and slung his arms over their shoulders — he was barely conscious and had to be half-carried, half-dragged down to the skyship. As they got closer, they could hear shouting and ropes rattling through deadeyes as the sails were raised, and then Finny calling, 'Cast off! Close hatches!'

'Got — to — hurry,' Davin muttered. 'Leaving.'

Kiall tried to increase the pace but Maya's side of the path was rough and uneven, and he feared tipping them all over. Ahead of them, he made out the bottom door into the hold, a black hole against the side of the ship, that would close any moment. There! He was sure it was moving; there must be a winch on the upper deck. With a strength that came from the desperate fear of being left to die in this terrible place, Kiall surged forward, carrying

Davin and Maya with him. He heard Maya stumble and curse but she didn't fall, and he kept going.

When they reached the door, it was halfway up, like a drawbridge closing the way into the castle forever. 'Hold Davin up,' he told Maya, and leapt onto the door, turning swiftly to reach down for Davin's arm to haul him up. Kiall thought his arm would be wrenched out of its socket, but there was no time to groan. Maya still stood below him on the ground, and the rising door was taking him further away from her.

'Jump!' he snapped, and without hesitating she crouched, then launched herself upwards, arms stretching up to his hands. For a moment, he thought he'd missed her, then his fingers closed around her wrists and he pulled backwards as hard as he could. She was as heavy as a small elephant, it seemed, but he leaned back and used his own body like a counterweight.

'Ooommphhh.' Maya slid up and over the edge of the door, and together they fell backwards into the hold, but Maya came to a sudden stop. 'Curses!' she said. 'My boot is caught.' She jerked her foot down but the door was nearly closed and the boot was caught fast.

'Get your foot out — quick,' Kiall said. A picture of Maya's foot crushed in the door flashed through his mind and he felt sick. He wasn't sure she heard him but a couple of seconds later her foot popped out of the boot and she landed on top of him.

'Dad-fangled door,' she said. 'These are my favourite boots. What am I going to do with one boot?'

Kiall started grinning and Maya looked at him. 'What's so funny, stupid brother?' Then she giggled and in an instant they were both laughing so hard they had to lie down on the deck.

'My stomach hurts,' Kiall said when they finally calmed down. 'I can't remember the last time we did that.'

'Not since you cut off half of Papa's moustache while he was asleep.'

That set them giggling again, until Kiall said, 'I wonder if Papa is still in the dungeon.'

Maya frowned. 'I doubt Mama would have found the money to free him.' 'And now we don't have any either.' He pointed at Davin who lay on the deck near them, breathing heavily, his face a white oval in the dark hold. 'We carried him on board and left the gold behind! We should have left him. Papa will never be freed now.'

'Calm down, Kiall,' Maya said. She fumbled with her belt, uncinched it and pulled a small sack out from under her shirt. The sack's drawstring was hooked around her neck; she took it off and dropped it on the floor with a loud clunk. 'You don't honestly think I would've left our treasure behind, do you? After what we've been through?'

Joy flooded through Kiall like a rushing blue wave. He grabbed Maya and hugged her tightly. 'I'll say it again, little sister. You are amazing.'

'Enough of the little,' she grumbled. 'You are only five minutes older than me, and much less intelligent.'

Davin moaned and they both turned to tend to him. Maya checked his chest wound and said, 'It's opened up again. We need to undo this wrapping and tighten it somehow.'

Kiall glanced around the hold. 'Before we do that, we have to find somewhere to hide. If a sky pirate comes down here for any reason — or even when they reach Quentaris — they will likely throw us overboard.'

'Or take us back to Blackwine,' Maya said grimly.

'I'll try to staunch Davin's bleeding. You look around.'

Kiall started at the bow, where he and Maya had hidden under black sheets, and worked his way back to the stern, hoping there would be storage areas or at least some boxes, but there was nothing. The hold was bare and open; the only advantage they had was that there was no lighting of any kind. They could huddle in the farthest, darkest corner, keeping totally still. If the sky pirates came straight down to the ladder, they might escape detection. When he reported back to Maya, she grimaced. 'We'll have to hope that luck is on our side for once. It's not as if we've used it all up — we've had none!'

They carried Davin to a corner in the stern and re-tied his wrapping, trying not to worry too much about the fresh blood that leaked unremittingly from the gash.

As they settled back against the hull, a faint wall of green light appeared at the bow and travelled down the hold, passing over them and disappearing.

'That was the rift,' Kiall said, excitement fizzing inside him. 'We're nearly home!'

'Yes,' said Maya. 'All we have to do now is get off this ship without being seen and climb down a rope ladder carrying a dead weight between us.' She grinned at Kiall. 'Shouldn't be too difficult, should it?'

9
Air and
Water

KIALL AND MAYA WERE too nervous to
sleep, although Kiall knew he couldn't
have slept anyway. He'd kept from Maya
the seriousness of his foot injury, and was having
second thoughts. She was relying on him to help
with Davin and get them safely off the skyship, but
he doubted he could climb down the swaying
ladder. Now that they were sitting down, resting,
he could tell there was something very wrong. The

throbbing consumed his whole foot and had moved halfway up his leg. When he finally was able to cut his boot off, he believed his foot may well explode, and what was even worse was the terrible smell. If he didn't know better, he would have said the deadly cat was on the skyship with them — instead, it was his foot turning gangrenous.

'Do you think that horrible cat has been in this hold?' Maya said, wrinkling her nose.

Kiall felt cold all over. 'Um ... quite possibly,' he said, shifting his foot away from Maya. No, he didn't want her to know. They had enough to worry about.

It didn't seem long before the humming noise changed to a throatier rumble and boots thumped across the deck. 'We must be out of the cave,' Kiall said. 'Soon they'll be coming down to use the ladder, so get ready.'

'For what? We'll be pretending to be statues, that's all.'

'Anything could happen. Just be ready.'

Maya scowled but didn't answer back. They sat in silence in the darkness, waiting, trying not to think about what might happen if the pirates saw them. If they were on their way to plunder in the city, they'd kill the trio to keep them quiet. Davin was in no condition to talk their way out, even if Finny would listen to him.

More footsteps overhead, some shouting, then, in the distance, a bell ringing. Closer, another bell tolled over and over like an echo. 'The ship's been seen,' Kiall said. 'Those are the Quentaris warning bells.'

'But ...' Maya looked up. 'The pirates — they'll turn around and go back. How are we going to get off?' She leapt up. 'We have to lower the ladder and climb down. Even if we don't get close enough to the ground until we're back in the cave, we've got to get off this thing!'

'How are we going to get him down the ladder?' Kiall jerked his head at Davin.

'I don't know!' Maya said shrilly. She headed to the hatch and forced it open, then unrolled the ladder. It tumbled out into the darkness. Kiall hauled Davin to his feet and dragged him across the hold.

As the shouting and thumping on the upper deck got louder, Kiall heard soft thuds against the side of the ship. The floor lurched and the ship began to turn, but slowly, while more thuds sounded throughout the hull.

'What is that?' Maya said. 'Arrows? Why are they wasting arrows on a huge ship like this?' She knelt by the hatch and stuck her head through the hole. 'Oh my —' She drew back so quickly that she toppled over.

'What? What's happening?' Kiall said, panic rising in his throat.

'They're shooting fire arrows,' Maya said. 'Lots of them. We're on fire, in about forty different places.'

'The pirates will never make it back to the cave. We'll probably crash.' He lowered Davin to the floor and peered through the hatch opening. The Quentarans had lit beacon fires on some of the rooftops, probably to provide instant flame for the arrows. He could see that the ladder was about thirty feet above the highest roofs.

'It's still too high,' he said. 'And if we climb down and hang on until we get closer, we'll probably get fired on by our own guards.'

It was hopeless. Either way, they were going to die.

'Can you feel that?' Maya said. She leant forward and peered out again.

'What?'

'We're going down — look.'

Kiall looked out. She was right. The ladder was now only a few feet above the roofs. 'We'll still get shot at. But look where we're heading.'

'Back to the — oh, we're near the wharves. And still dropping.' She grinned. 'The pirates are landing their ship in the harbour. They must think it's the softest landing, and it'll put the fires out.'

'There'll be no soft landing,' Kiall said. 'We're travelling too fast. If we survive the crash, we'll have to be ready to swim.' He pointed at the stern. Flames had eaten their way through the hull. 'The water will rush in and put the fire out, but we'll need to escape that way. And be swift about it.'

They moved back towards the stern and sat down, bracing themselves against the side, wedging Davin between them. 'Kiall,' Maya said.

'What?'

'If you get out and I don't, tell Mama and Papa I love them.'

'You'll be fine,' Kiall said, trying to find a place to rest his foot that didn't make him want to scream.

'And tell Mama that I'm sorry I never learned to sew properly, but it just bored me to tears.'

There was a great shout from above, then the ship hit the water with an enormous, juddering crash. Timber snapped and cracked, pieces of the hull flew around the hold, some hitting them as they were flung across the floor. Maya slid in a heap to the other side; Kiall kept a grip on Davin and ducked the debris. At first there was no water, then it began to rush in through the burned-out stern, washing over them and flowing to the bow, deepening by the second.

Kiall struggled up but his foot gave way and he fell again. A few seconds later, Maya was there. She dragged him up. 'Come on! Grab Davin. Pull him if you have to.' They grasped Davin's hands and started towards the stern; he was floating, which made it easier. Kiall stumbled several times, the stabbing pain up past his knee, but Maya was struggling too. The force of the water was so great that they couldn't reach the hole, and were being continually pushed backwards.

'Wait,' Kiall gasped. 'When the hold is nearly full, we can swim out.' Surely swimming would be easier than walking.

'Don't let Davin go,' Maya said.

'I won't,' Kiall said, although right then he wished they'd left the boy behind. Just as he'd suspected, Davin might be the death of all of them, even if not in the way he had originally thought.

The water slowed, and Kiall said, 'Now. Swim for your life!' Together they paddled to the hole, took deep breaths, grasped the sides and propelled themselves through, pulling Davin with them. The water was like black ink and Kiall prayed that they weren't too deep. He could hold his breath for a fair while, but Davin wasn't even conscious of what was happening. He would be breathing in water.

As if he knew what Kiall was thinking, Davin bucked in his grip, fighting the unexpected intake of water. Kiall couldn't see where Maya was. They had to get the boy to the surface before he drowned!

As his head broke the water, Kiall felt Davin go slack. Was it too late? He turned Davin on his back but he couldn't tell if he was breathing. Where were they? Gods, they were much further out in the harbour than he'd expected. How were they going to get to shore with a dying boy?

Pieces of broken wood and fragments of burnt sail floated around him. The body of a sky pirate bobbed to the surface not far away.

Where was Maya?

Panic clutched at Kiall's guts. She had been right with him. How could she have disappeared? Was she hurt? She couldn't be drowning — she had always been a better swimmer than he. He let Davin go and prepared to dive down to look for Maya.

'Ahoy there!'

Kiall jerked around to find a longboat not twenty feet away. In the bow, a man stood holding a lantern and a long pole with a hook on it. Two others leaned over the side, sifting through the debris for salvage. 'Over here,' Kiall called as loudly as he could, pushing Davin's body towards them.

As the boat reached him and hands came down to lift him in, he said, 'No, take the boy. He's drowned. You have to save him.'

'Get the boy in,' the lantern man ordered. 'Turn him over, squeeze the water out of him.'

Kiall batted away the hands that came down again. He searched desperately in the dark water for Maya. 'My sister — she's still down there. I have to save her.' He took a deep breath, ready to plunge down into the depths.

A few feet away, water boiled and two hands thrashed about, then Maya's face popped up, her mouth open as she sucked in great gulps of air. 'Kiall — help.'

Kiall swam towards her as fast as he could and

reached his arms around her, holding her up in the water while he kicked hard, barely feeling the pain in his foot. Within a few seconds, the longboat reached them and they were both hauled in like large fish. The men who had hold of Maya grunted with the effort.

In the bottom of the boat, Kiall said, 'What happened? I thought you had drowned.'

'I had a bit more to carry up than you,' she muttered in his ear. 'I told you I wasn't going to leave it behind.' She patted the sack.

'You could have died!' he spluttered.

'Don't worry. If it had really weighed me down, I would have left it there. And come out diving tomorrow to retrieve it, of course.'

'Oh, of course,' Kiall said dryly.

The man with the lantern sitting in the bow began asking questions. 'What were you doing on a skyship? What land are you from? Are you pirates?'

'We're from Quentaris,' Maya said. 'We're not pirates.'

'We are Kiall and Maya Tigran,' Kiall said. 'Of the Tigran family, merchants of fine goods — the best, in fact.'

The man held his lantern a little higher. 'Is that

right? You look like the poorest of beggars. And you don't smell too good either.'

One of the other men added, 'Your parents will no doubt be willing to pay a reward for rescuing you, all the same.'

Kiall opened his mouth to argue, then thought better of it. 'You will have to speak to them,' was all he said.

Behind them, Davin was coughing and trying to sit up. 'He's injured,' Maya told the men. 'A sword cut across his chest. He needs to go to the hospital.'

'Just as well it's near the docks,' said one of the men. 'He's bleeding bad.'

At the hospital, Davin was rushed off to the healers while two physicians tied cloths over their faces before they attempted to cut Kiall's boot off his foot. Kiall closed his eyes. He didn't want to see what his foot looked like, especially if it meant he might lose it. A picture of himself hobbling around on a wooden leg with a walking stick had begun to haunt him.

Maya had no such qualms. She hid her sack under the bed, and peered at his leg as they cut the boot apart. Kiall heard her gasp. 'How long has it been like this?'

'A while.'

'Why didn't you tell me?'

'What good would it have done?' Kiall said.

'I could have bled you, or cleaned it, or … or …'
Her face was pale. 'Can you save it?' she asked the
physicians.

Kiall couldn't stand the suspense. He sat up and
looked at his foot, and then had to swallow hard to
stop from vomiting. One of the physicians poked at
the purple, swollen mass and a fountain of yellow
pus spurted out. The physicians marvelled and
whispered and finally said, 'We will start immedi-
ate treatment but it looks to be draining naturally.
We think you will recover almost totally. Perhaps a
small limp.'

Kiall sagged back in relief. A small limp. He
could cope with that.

Maya went away for a short time while the physicians worked on his foot, and when she returned
she said, 'They have sent for Mama, and she is
bringing dry clothes. Davin is out of danger, and we
have a sack of treasure with which to save Papa.'
She grinned and squeezed Kiall's arm. 'We did it!'

At a sharp cough behind them, they both
turned. Commander Storm of the City Watch stood

in the doorway, her green eyes narrowed. 'I would like to know exactly what you have done. You two have some serious questions to answer.'

Kiall nodded. The story of how they came to be on a skyship, where they had been and what had happened would have to be told to the commander first, then to Papa and Mama.

And then maybe he'd go and tell the tale to Rad de La'rel as well.

Epilogue

YSABEL TIGRAN SAILED INTO the hospital room like a warship ready for battle, her eyes flashing dangerously. Kiall shrank down in his bed, wondering if he could pretend to be unconscious. His mother was about to give him the tongue-lashing of his life.

Then he spotted someone else behind her.

'Papa!' Kiall's mouth hung open in disbelief.

Maya leapt up from her chair and flung her arms around her father. 'They let you out to see us.'

Paolo hugged his daughter, then stepped over to Kiall's bed. Ysabel joined him and they both frowned down at Kiall.

'How in the heavens did you get kidnapped by sky pirates?' Paolo demanded.

'I've been worried sick about you!' Ysabel said. 'Have you been taking care of your sister?'

'I think she took care of me,' Kiall said, grinning.

'This is not funny,' Paolo snapped. 'We thought you had been abducted as slaves.'

'We were trying to find treasure, Papa,' Kiall said. 'To get you out of the dungeon and pay off the business debts. And guess what? We —'

'There is no need,' Paolo interrupted. 'I am free, and the culprits are behind bars instead.'

Ysabel took her husband's hand.

Paolo grimaced. 'A nephew of Tash Morley's came forward and gave evidence. It turned out that the saboteurs are cousins of Morley's, but of course he knew absolutely nothing about their trickery.'

'So you're free,' Maya said. 'And we can help you rebuild the business with our —'

'The scandal over the sabotage created such a

commotion among all the businesses that our creditors have waived all our debts,' Paolo said. 'I have one ship left. It came in safely yesterday filled with valuable spices and silk. It will ensure our business is off to a new start. And this time I will make strong partnerships with our business friends that should avoid future treachery.'

'So you don't actually need our ...' Kiall stopped and looked at Maya.

'That's wonderful, Papa,' Maya said. 'And one day Kiall and I plan to have a merchant house to rival yours. Maya Imports.'

'Kiall Imports!' Kiall said.

'Whose sack is it?' Maya asked, hands on hips. Then she and Kiall burst out laughing, leaving their parents to stare from one to the other with puzzled faces.

THE QUENTARIS CHRONICLES

Rifts through Quentaris

Karen R. Brooks

Adyren Worthing longs to be anything other than what she is: an apprentice in the League of Bibliophiles. But master thief does not figure in her daydreams. When she is accused of stealing, no one, not even her own family, believes her claims of innocence. To uncover the truth, she must travel to another world and discover the terrible secret of her birth.

Karen R. Brooks is a senior lecturer in popular culture at the University of the Sunshine Coast. She is the author of the popular Cassandra Klein series, which includes *It's Time, Cassandra Klein, The Gaze of the Gorgon, The Book of Night* and *The Kurs of Atlantis*, all published by Lothian Books.

ISBN 0 7344 0745 9

The Plague of Quentaris

Gary Crew

But on the last day of the Three-Day Dark, some said they saw a shape in the starry sky. A black void, where no star shone. A void in the shape of a rat ...

Is this a warning of fantastical events to befall Quentaris? What part do the rat children, Anton and Vega, play in this horror? Is this the final calamity that will destroy the mighty city?

Gary Crew is one of Australia's most awarded authors, winning the Children's Book Coucil of Australia Book of the Year award four times. He is internationally acclaimed for his fantasy novels and illustrated books, including the best-selling *Strange Objects* and *The Watertower*.

0 7344 0773 4

Princess of Shadows

Paul Collins

When a dreadful curse descends on Quentaris, Tamaika uncovers an ancient book that bestows magical powers on the finder. She transforms into the mythical Princess of Shadows, but is she strong enough to control such power? And will Tamaika be able to lift the curse that turns citizens into stone?

Paul Collins has been short-listed for many Australian science fiction and fantasy awards, and has won the Aurealis, William Atheling and inaugural Peter McNamara awards. His books include *The Great Ferret Race*, *Dragonlinks*, *Swords of Quentaris*, *Slaves of Quentaris* and *Dragonlords of Quentaris*.

ISBN 0 7344 0799 8

The Cat Dreamer

Isobelle Carmody

A strange, mind-numbing fog shrouds Quentaris and a cat that is more than it seems enters the city. It is a dangerous time in Quentaris. Before it is over, the city and its magical rift caves will face destruction. It is up to Igorik and the girl who visits him in his dreeams to do all they can to save Quentaris and its inhabitants.

Isobelle Carmody is a prolific science fiction and fantasy writer of many award-winning books. These include *Dreamwalker*, *Journey frm the Centre of the Earth* and *Angel Fever*, her first book in the Quentaris Chronicles. Isobelle is currently workiing on the final book in the Obernewtyn Chronicles.

ISBN 0 7344 0762 9

Nightmare in Quentaris

Michael Pryor

Arna Greentower and her Old Tree Guesthouse, are experiencing difficult times. Employees mysteriously disappear, deliveries go astray and business is faltering. Arna's foster-daughter Nisha, a fire magician, and her friend Tal are determined to uncover the secrets behind a forbidden room in the guesthouse and the memory-eating powers of its menacing occupant. But he is only one of Arna's enemies. Former business rival and fugitive Gorv is back in Quentaris and looking for revenge.

Michael Pryor is the popular author of many award-winning novels and short stories, including *Quentaris in Flames*, *Beneath Quentaris* and *Stones of Quentaris*. Michael lives in Melbourne with his wife Wendy and two daughters, Celeste and Ruby.

ISBN 0 7344 0774 2

The Murderers' Apprentice

Pamela Freeman

Like her father and mother before her, Merrith is apprenticed to become an assassin with the Murderers' Guild. But Merrith is hopeless with a dagger and sword, inept at mixing poison and isn't quite okay with the idea of killing people anyway. Merrith's talents, it seems, lie elsewhere.

Just as she is due to begin her apprenticeship, the Guild of Soothsayers instruct Merrith to join an expedition to the rift caves, and it comes with a warning: if she fails to go, Quentaris will be destroyed.

Can Merrith save Quentaris from devious Sorrell, the leader of the expedition? And will she discover her true vocation and escape her supposed destiny as a professional murderess?

Pamela Freeman started writing stories for children in the early 1990s while she was a scriptwriter at the ABC. Her work, which includes *The Willow Tree's Daughter, Victor's Quest* and *Pole to Pole*, has been short-listed for the NSW Premier's Literary Awards, the Children's Book Council Book of the Year Award for Younger Readers and the Koala Awards. Pamela grew up in Sydney's western suburbs and now lives in the inner-city with her husband and young son.

ISBN 0 7344 0800 5

Stolen Children of Quentaris

Gary Crew

Why did Nordian traders kidnap children from the city of Quentaris? Did they really sell them to the hideous Rodentia, rat king of the Trollantan Mountains? In this spellbinding prequel to *The Plague of Quentaris*, best-selling author Gary Crew reveals all ...

Gary Crew is one of Australia's most awarded authors, winning the Children's Book Council of Australia Book of the Year four times. He is internationally acclaimed for his fantasy novels and illustrated books, and is also the author of *The Plague of Quentaris*.

ISBN 0 7344 0880 3